LAST SHOT

Other books by David Skuy

Rocket Blues

Undergrounders

The Game Time series:

Off the Crossbar

Rebel Power Play

Making the Cut

Overtime

Double Shift

LAST SHOT

David Skuy

Scholastic Canada Ltd.
Toronto New York London Auckland Sydney
Mexico City New Delhi Hong Kong Buenos Aires

Scholastic Canada Ltd.
604 King Street West, Toronto, Ontario M5V 1E1, Canada
Scholastic Inc.
557 Broadway, New York, NY 10012, USA
Scholastic Australia Pty Limited
PO Box 579, Gosford, NSW 2250, Australia
Scholastic New Zealand Limited
Private Bag 94407, Botany, Manukau 2163, New Zealand
Scholastic Children's Books
Euston House, 24 Eversholt Street, London NW1 1DB, UK

www.scholastic.ca

Library and Archives Canada Cataloguing in Publication
Skuy, David, 1963-, author
        Last shot / David Skuy.
Sequel to: Rocket blues.
Issued in print and electronic formats.
ISBN 978-1-4431-4669-2 (paperback).--ISBN 978-1-4431-4670-8
(html).-- ISBN 978-1-4431-4671-5 (Apple edition)
        I. Title.
PS8637.K72L38 2015   jC813'.6   C2015-904596-7
                                              C2015-904597-5

Cover photo © Volkova Irina/Shutterstock.com

6 5 4 3 2 1   Printed in Canada 139   15 16 17 18 19

*To the kids who play the game
for all the right reasons.*

CHAPTER 1

Feedback crackled like thunder over the arena's loud-speaker. The people in front of him nearly jumped out of their seats. Rocket didn't flinch. Six hours slouched in this spot, waiting for his name to be called, had numbed his body and his nerves.

Yesterday he'd come for his friends, Tyler and Adam, and he'd been stoked when they were drafted. Ty went fifth in round one to the London Knights. The Oshawa Generals grabbed Adam early in round two, with the third pick. Rocket had known he wouldn't go in the first three rounds.

The three of them had been obsessed with the Ontario Hockey League draft for weeks, though Rocket pretended to be low-key. He'd scored thirty-nine goals in midget last season, fourth highest in the league. A few scouts had called Coach Sonia to ask about him. Still, she had warned Rocket not to go to the draft.

"It could be awful," she said. "You might sit in the stands for two days and not get drafted. Stay home and wait to hear from the team that picks you."

Good advice. Too bad he'd ignored it. In the past he would have just checked online, but the OHL had decided to do it live in an arena, like they had years ago. But round after round — nothing. Each time a general manager went up to the mic, Rocket's heart started to beat a little faster.

Another name was called out — not his.

"Cool news about Tyler and Adam."

Rocket looked up at hearing his friends mentioned. Two men had taken a seat across the aisle. The man closest to him wore a suit and sunglasses with thick black rims. A large gold watch caught the light every so often as the man gestured with his hands. The second man was younger, thickset, wearing track pants, a hoodie and running shoes.

The first man was Mr. Cole and the second was Coach Barker.

Rocket quickly turned away so they wouldn't see his face. Barker had cut Rocket from the Oakmont Huskies years ago. Cole had been the team's sponsor. Rocket didn't have fond memories of either of them.

"I should be down on that floor," Barker said. "I'm good at working trades and stuff like that."

"I just bought the team," Cole said. "I don't want to rock the boat. You'll come on as an assistant coach this year."

"Well, we got to take care of that power play, and your team is way too small. We need some big bodies to cycle in the corners, and I want my defencemen to punish guys who try to get to the net," Barker said.

Rocket had played for the AAA Oakmont Huskies for three years, but in his bantam year, Cole had brought in Barker as a paid coach. Rocket still remembered sitting in the dressing room after the tryout, laughing and joking with Ty and Ad-man. He'd thought he was a lock to make the team. He was the team's lead scorer, and the Huskies had just won the league championship. The manager had read the names out, and Rocket had to sit, humiliated, as it became clear he'd been cut, just like that, in front of everyone.

The hurt had never gone away.

Barker had cut him because he was too small.

And now, years later, that was likely the reason he was still sitting here, not drafted.

Despite his talent, OHL hockey teams couldn't see beyond his size.

Rocket would prove them wrong. He had so far.

Thirty-nine goals last season!

If he didn't get drafted, he'd have to try again next year. It was possible, but if he didn't get any bigger, it wasn't likely. He looked at the scoreboard. Round fifteen was about to start — the last. Twenty teams, fifteen rounds.

Would all the championship teams, the goals and assists, the years of training, early morning runs and shooting a tennis ball against the wall at the back of his apartment count for nothing?

"I like a few of the kids on the team," Barker was saying. "You have that Nugent kid on D. He's a banger. I can develop him. Watch me. And I really like that Ferguson. Kid's got jam."

"That he does." Cole slapped Barker on the side of the leg and stood up. "Anyway, I should get back down there for the final round. Let's circle back tomorrow. I'll introduce you to the staff and we can talk about training camp."

"Sounds great. Looking forward to it."

As Cole left, Barker pulled out his phone and made a call.

"Yeah, I just spoke to him. Went well. I'm irritated that I couldn't help with the draft, but I get it. Cole doesn't want to step on any toes. But I'm perfectly positioned to take over. Only Cole would buy such a useless team. Guess he's got more money than brains. I heard he spent seven million. He's got no patience. The team will start losing, and he'll name me head coach . . ."

How much money did Cole have? Seven million! That was ridiculous.

Rocket wondered what team it was. Then he felt sorry for whoever had to play for Barker. Ty and Adman had hated him. Rocket brought his feet up on the top of the seat in front of him and gripped his knees. He let himself relax. Barker wouldn't recognize him — too long ago.

For the umpteenth time, he considered his options. Play Junior A or B, or major midget, and get drafted next year. That was the best-case scenario. If he didn't get drafted next year, either, he could go to an OHL training camp and try to make it as a free agent. Not the best plan — that almost never happened.

He knew the stats.

The rink had been packed this morning, families jumping up and cheering whenever their lucky kid was named. Hour after hour passed, family after family celebrated — hugs and kisses everywhere — but here he was, sitting alone, round fifteen. Maybe Coach Sonia had been trying to tell him that he wasn't going to be drafted. Maybe the scouts had told her.

All his life he'd dreamed of playing in the NHL. The OHL was the first step — the Big O.

Ty and Adam had already made it. No surprise there. Their parents were rich, and his friends seemed to get everything they wanted: elite hockey camps, top-of-the-line equipment, tropical vacations, the latest phones and tech. Rocket didn't care so much about that. But Ty and Adam also had the one thing he'd give anything for: they had the size.

The loudspeaker boomed again. "The Barrie Colts will pick first in the fifteenth round, having obtained the Sault Ste. Marie Greyhounds' pick."

A general manager approached the podium. "The Barrie Colts select Dominique Jeffries."

"They picked that Jeffries," Barker said in his phone. "I know the kid. He's a stiff. Can barely skate. Anyway, I gotta go. I'll call you back."

Rocket gripped his knees tighter and waited as five more picks went by. His lower back began to hurt and his neck began to ache. He remained perfectly still.

"The Axton Axmen have the next pick."

The Axmen hadn't done well last year. They'd traded up and got the third pick overall, an American named Aaron Cashman. Rocket had never played against him, but he knew the name.

A tall, broad-shouldered man with a flattened nose and a slight, manicured beard took the stage and grabbed the mic. After sitting in the rink for two days, Rocket had learned the names of most of the general managers. This was Jamie Gold. Rocket had looked him up. He'd actually played in the NHL.

"The Axton Axmen will take . . ." Gold stared at his iPad. "The Axmen take . . . Brent . . . Hold on." He paused to put on his glasses.

Rocket leaned his head back and stared up at the ceiling. He should go home.

"Sorry about that," Gold said. "The Axton Axmen take Bryan Rockwood."

The arena started to spin and all the lights seemed to have gone dim.

"Bryan Rockwood, taken by the Axton Axmen," a voice announced over the loudspeaker.

Rocket rose unsteadily and shuffled to the aisle. His head was spinning so fast he felt like he'd just come off a wicked rollercoaster.

"The Rocket gets drafted." Barker laughed as he went by. "I think you were this size in bantam."

Rocket ignored him and continued down the stairs — slowly. He didn't trust his legs.

Get stoked, he told himself. Not the round you wanted, but you got drafted. Someone wants you.

Axton might not be a bad team, either, not with that Cashman.

Rocket walked through the gate and onto the concrete pad. It felt weird to be in a hockey rink without ice. A spattering of applause filtered down from the few remaining people in the stands.

Rocket looked up toward the stage. The general manager had gone back to the team's table already. Another man was walking toward Rocket, hand outstretched.

"Welcome to the Axmen," he said as Rocket shook

his hand. "My name's Bradley Washington. I'm the assistant coach. I saw you play a few times last year. Love your skating and vision — and your work ethic."

"Thanks. I'm . . . happy to be drafted by Axton." Rocket figured that was the right thing to say.

"Come on over to the table and meet everyone," Washington said.

Two men were seated there, the general manager, Gold, and a smaller man wearing a loose-fitting suit, his tie half undone. His dark brown eyes pierced into Rocket, but he said nothing and went back to looking at his computer screen.

"Gentlemen," Washington said, "I'd like to introduce Bryan Rockwood. Bryan, this is Jamie Gold. He's our GM and an owner."

Gold looked Rocket up and down. He pointed a pen at himself. "Like he said, owner of the Axton Axmen, team president and general manager — so welcome. I . . . uh . . . I've been where you are now, drafted late, and I went to the Battalion as a nobody. But I fought for every minute of ice time — and fought most of the guys in the league. Didn't let no one stop me — no one — and I played two years in the NHL. I learned that hockey's about grit and guts and determination, and that's what Axmen hockey is going to be: tough and physical. We'll dominate in all four corners — and on the scoreboard." He checked himself. "I sort of like my boys to have some meat on their bones. You're, uh, not the biggest cup of coffee I've ever seen."

He laughed. Washington seemed embarrassed. The other man wasn't paying attention.

"I'll tell you this," Gold continued. "One of us here

really wanted to draft you — and it wasn't me. It was the fifteenth round, so I didn't care. Hopefully, you'll prove me wrong. Anyway, we want you to come to camp and show us why you deserve to be an Axton Axman. That's an honour, believe me. I hope you can live up to it."

Washington smiled uneasily. "Bryan, this is our coach, the legendary J.J. Alvo."

Alvo looked up. For the briefest of moments, his eyes warmed up. "See you at the end of the summer for training camp, Bryan," he said. His eyes went back to his screen.

Washington gave Rocket a large white envelope with *Axton Axmen* printed on the front in bright red lettering. "Everything you need to know about training camp is in there, along with information about billeting with a family, school choices and expense information," he said. "Training camp starts the last week in August. We're going with a three-day camp this year. Come in shape and ready to compete. Sound good?"

Rocket's head had barely stopped spinning the entire time. It was all he could do to nod.

"The London Knights select . . ."

Washington put an arm around Rocket's shoulders and led him toward the stands. "Go celebrate with your family." He slipped a card into Rocket's hand. "Give me a call if you have any questions, anything at all. I'd be glad to speak to your mom or dad. It's a big step for kids: leaving home, changing schools and playing in the major juniors, all at the same time. Just remember, not too many sixteen-year-olds make it through the training camp, so you need to manage your expectations." A big smile crept across his face. "But today you got drafted, Bryan. Be happy! Go enjoy yourself and we'll talk soon."

They shook hands and Rocket left the floor.

Not the biggest cup of coffee. Rocket thought about Gold. The Axmen's GM had played for Boston, the New York Rangers and then the St. Louis Blues. Not much of a player, more like a journeyman, and a bit of a goon, but an NHLer.

Two years in the NHL — you could live off that money forever, Rocket thought. He could get his mom out of their nasty apartment building and buy her a house in a nice neighbourhood. He'd still have enough to pay for Maddy's university — and get her a house, too.

He headed into the stands. Unfortunately, Barker was standing by the exit, leaning against the wall, grinning.

"Congrats, Rockwood," he said. "I got to admit, I didn't think you still played and I certainly didn't expect you to get drafted. Last round . . ." He laughed.

Rocket wasn't going to let Barker ruin this for him.

"Don't worry about me," he said.

Barker tilted his head back. "Here's some advice. Quit while you're still in one piece. The OHL is for big boys — and I mean big. You . . . ?" He shook his head. "I cut you in bantam because you were too small — and I let myself be talked into asking you back. Trust me, I was against it, and no one was happier when you said no. I coach in the OHL now, so listen up. Hockey's done for you. You didn't grow. Not your fault. You just didn't."

"One man's opinion," Rocket said.

"Just being honest. Sorry. That's me. I tell it like it is," Barker said.

"I'm sure you'll be as bad a coach in the OHL as you were with the Huskies," Rocket said. Then he walked past Barker, through the exit and over to the escalator.

The Axton Axmen! Barker could mock him all he liked, but Rocket had been drafted, and if he made the cut at training camp, it would be a huge step toward the NHL. He'd establish himself as a serious player and put an end to the questions about his size.

Gold said he'd fought for every minute of ice time. Rocket would do more than that. He'd fight for every second.

CHAPTER 2

"Forty-eight, forty-nine, fifty."

Rocket leapt up in the air to finish his last burpee.

"Come on, André," he said to the boy next to him. "You're slacking off again."

André growled and finished his last five burpees. He ran a hand through his thick blond hair. "Calm down. You're making me look bad. We finished yet?"

Rocket nodded. "As soon as we do our cool-down jog."

André groaned, but he fell in beside Rocket, and they set off down the path that ran around the park. A light rain began to fall.

"Did you order this rain to punish me for being out of shape?" André said.

"It's part of the cool-down." Rocket ducked under a tree branch. "This reminds me of my first tryout with the Bowmont Blues, after the Huskies cut me. I came here for a run, and it was raining pretty good."

André had been the Blues' captain. They'd stayed friends, even though they were no longer teammates and André lived on the other side of the city. Usually they met somewhere in between their places, like for a movie or just to hang, or he went to André's.

Rocket never really invited people over to his apartment. His school was in a really nice area, so his friends were rich, at least compared to him. He always figured they'd be too freaked out to come to his rundown neighbourhood — and he was embarrassed about where he lived.

Today, André had sent a text asking him what he was doing. When Rocket said he was training, André surprised him by saying he'd come over. Rocket suggested another spot, like his school, which was about forty-five minutes away. But André had made a joke about Rocket's time being too valuable because he had training camp in a week. He'd insisted on meeting Rocket here.

"It's amazing to think the Blues led to you being drafted to the OHL. I'm so stoked for you," André said.

"It was the last round."

"Once they see you play, you'll make it."

"Hope so. I told you about their GM."

"That Gold guy?"

"Yeah. He's into big, tough guys. I know I'm not the biggest guy in the world. How can I forget? Everyone tells me that a hundred times a day."

"Reminds me: Rocket, you're not the biggest guy in the world."

"Hardy-har-har."

"It's not the end of the world if you don't make it."

"It's only sort of the end," Rocket joked.

"We're going around again?"

Rocket held up four fingers. He always finished off

with five laps. "I guess going down a level to Junior A wouldn't be the worst. Lots of guys do and still play for their OHL team the next year," he said.

They ducked under the branch again and rounded the corner.

"But," Rocket continued, "if I can make it this year, I'm that much closer to the NHL. I'll be seen as a real prospect. Scouts will take notice. I got to bring it — big time. I can't give the Axmen any excuse not to add me to the roster."

They finished another lap.

"How do they look this year?" André said.

"Lots of turnover. They had a veteran team, only one sixteen-year-old. Didn't do too well the past couple years, but they used to be pretty good. Their number-one pick is a hotshot from Michigan."

"Sounds like there's a spot up for grabs for a fancy-pants scoring machine named Rocket," André said.

Rocket laughed. "I'd feel better if you were the GM."

"You'd be on the bench. Your ego is out of control."

"I wouldn't play for a hack like you, anyway—"

"Watch out!" André said as they both skidded to a stop. They just managed to avoid two boys who'd cut through some bushes to cross the park.

Rocket knew them. Bad dudes. They wore faded jean jackets with *Brigade* written across the back and had bandanas tied around their right arms. One of them, Connor, was basically a gangbanger. He'd dropped out of school, and Rocket knew he hung out at the Grove, the bar around the corner, even though he was only seventeen.

"Hey, Raja, check out these losers. You little boys lost?" Connor sneered.

Raja laughed.

Rocket wasn't worried, not with André there.

"Sorry. We're just running . . . training. See ya," Rocket said.

Connor knocked him to the ground with a vicious two-handed shove to his chest.

"Don't run into me next time," Connor growled.

"Yeah, no running into us," Raja said.

"Back off, bro," André said, taking a step toward Connor. No surprise that André wasn't scared. He was a big guy. He didn't live here, though. He didn't know who he was messing with, and he wouldn't have to deal with the consequences.

Rocket got to his feet.

"Back off or what?" Connor said.

"Come find out," André said calmly.

Connor moved toward André, who didn't budge. He towered above Connor.

"You're lucky we got to go," Connor said. "I see you around here again, your face is broken." He punched his fist into his palm.

Rocket bit his tongue. He didn't need trouble with these two.

"I got you figured as a total wimp — all talk," André said. "Break my face now."

"Relax, bulldog," Connor laughed. He flicked his chin at Rocket. "What are you going to do without your bodyguard around?"

So much for avoiding problems. "Whatever I want," Rocket said.

He'd lived here for most of his life. Rule number one: Show no fear.

Connor's eyes grew wide and he elbowed Raja. "Peewee is going to throw a hissy fit on us. He's all angry."

"Peewee angry," Raja said in a baby voice.

"You ever say anything original?" Rocket said to Raja.

Raja kept giggling.

"I'll see you around, Peewee," Connor said to Rocket. Then he glared at André. "Take a good long look in the mirror tonight. I'm going to destroy that face of yours." He turned to leave.

André shrugged. "Like I thought. He runs away."

Connor spun back. "You have a death wish? For real?"

"Apparently, you do, too," André said.

"We got to go, Connor," Raja said. He sounded nervous all of a sudden. "They're waiting for us. We shouldn't be late. They told us not to be late."

Connor pressed his lips together. "I so want to crack some heads." He pointed at André. "We'll *run* into each other again. Count on it."

This time he walked off. Raja, of course, followed.

"What was that?" André said.

Rocket felt himself flush. "Welcome to the neighbourhood."

"Those guys live around here?"

"Those guys . . . lots of other guys." No point hiding it. "I live there, in that apartment, the one with the grey wall."

Rocket knew what André was thinking: You actually live there, in that dump?

Instead of disgust, André's expression seemed

thoughtful. "I've heard this is a rough place. I know there are some gangs and stuff. I got to admit, my mom was a little freaked that I was coming here."

Rocket took it all in: the dark, crumbling apartment buildings, houses with boarded-up or broken windows, garbage strewn about. "That's sort of why I suggested the school."

"You training tomorrow?" André said suddenly.

"I guess — every day."

"I'll meet you back here tomorrow."

"We can meet at my school."

"Here," André said emphatically. "Those two weasels got on my nerves. Hopefully, they'll come around again."

"They definitely fit the weasel category." Rocket laughed, but the truth was he was scared of them. Connor and Raja weren't so tough on their own, but they were part of an actual gang. Some of the Brigades were older and pretty dangerous — you definitely wanted to avoid them. But how could a guy like André understand? He didn't have people like that in his neighbourhood.

André pulled out his water bottle. "Could I hit up your place for a refill? I'm about done."

"You could get some water at the corner store, on the way to the subway."

"Yeah, but I forgot my cash. Just got enough to get me home. Otherwise, I'm walking, and after that workout, I'm done exercising for the day. Bro, you'll be like Superman if you keep this workout up." He began to walk toward Rocket's apartment.

Rocket took a deep breath and ran to catch up.

"You make up your mind about who you're going to play for next season?" Rocket asked.

They crossed the street.

"I think I'm done," André said. "Grade eleven is a big year, and I have to focus on my grades. I might just fool around in a rec league with some buds."

Rocket was shocked. André could play. He really could. If he took it seriously, he might make a Junior B team, and then Junior A — even a university team.

"If you miss a year, then you may never make it back," Rocket said. They went into his building.

"Make it back to what?"

"To whatever. You have the skills," Rocket said. "You should play midget and go for the draft . . ." André was laughing. "Did I get funny?" Rocket asked.

The elevator came and they got in.

"Definitely not," André said. "You just don't get that most guys don't want to pay the price. You're willing to do it. I think you'd do almost anything to make it. Me? I'm not risking my body and a concussion and my education, especially when I know there's no point."

"You've got to have more confidence," Rocket said. "You get a free year of university for every year in the O. Did you know that?"

"I'm going to university anyway," André said.

Rocket felt stupid. André's family was rich. Of course, he was going to university. Rocket, on the other hand, wasn't going anywhere without hockey.

"Well . . . it's good for some guys," Rocket murmured.

The elevator opened. He heard some shouting from 1203. They were always arguing.

"I didn't mean it like that," André said.

Rocket took out his key, opened the door and went in.

"It's not going to happen for me," André said. "Too much of a long shot. For you, I get it. You can do it. It's worth the risk. You've got the talent."

Rocket suddenly felt tired. The odds of making the NHL were huge. Whenever he really thought about it, his stomach began to churn.

"You work off all that fat?" a voice called from the living room.

"Hi, Maddy," André called back.

The TV turned off and Maddy came into the hallway.

"You didn't tell me André was coming over," she said, sneaking an angry glance at Rocket.

"I didn't know," Rocket said.

Maddy was hard to understand. Why was she mad? He thought she liked André.

"He didn't think I'd get home in one piece," Rocket continued. "We met your friend Connor."

"What happened?" she said.

"Nothing," Rocket said. "We scared them away, but apparently André's face is about to be rearranged and I'm a dead man."

André began laughing.

"How is this funny?" Maddy gasped. "Those Brigade boys are the worst."

"More bark than bite," André said.

"It's easy for you to say. You're twice Bryan's size," Maddy said.

The room went silent.

Then Rocket and André went into hysterics. Rocket

was laughing so hard, he had to sit down in the hall.

"I forgot to tell you how small you are again," André sputtered.

"Why do I forget that boys are mentally damaged and aren't worth my time?" Maddy asked.

"Private joke. Sorry," André said.

Maddy threw her nose into the air. "I forgive you, but not Bryan. He's too stinky."

"Will you forgive me after my shower, sis?" Rocket said.

André looked puzzled. "Um, I thought you weren't actually brother and sister."

"We're not," Rocket said quickly. He shouldn't have said that. It was hard to explain. "Maddy used to live in this building, and then she moved in with us a few years ago."

He hoped that was enough. He couldn't remember what he'd told André about Maddy, and he didn't want to embarrass her.

"My mom left me," Maddy said in a determined voice. "She took off a few years ago, and then I lived with her ex-boyfriend for a while. He was a total jerk, so Risa invited me to live here. The sis-bro thing is our inside joke." She beamed a fake smile at Rocket.

Rocket was surprised. She never told people that.

"Must have been really tough," André said. He slid down the wall and joined Rocket on the floor.

Maddy shrugged, and then she sat down too. "I don't recommend it, but I'm okay. We're all okay. It's Risa I worry about. She has to work so hard and she has the two of us to support. We both have part-time jobs, but we don't make much."

"If I make the Axmen, all of my room and board, and a lot of other things, will be covered," Rocket said. He looked over at André. "That's another reason I have to make the team. Plus, my mom won't have to pay anything for me to play hockey, and I know it's a huge chunk of change for her."

The door opened.

"Hey, Mom," Rocket said.

Rocket's mother came in and put two plastic bags down. "Is there a reason you're all sitting on the floor in the hallway?" she said, her head tilted to the side.

"Because Bryan is small," Maddy said.

That set them off again.

Risa shook her head, laughing. "My goodness, André, I haven't seen you in years. Not since Bryan played on the Blues."

André stood up and shook her hand.

"Why don't you guys set up in the living room, and I can get dinner ready. Will you stay?" Risa asked André.

"That's nice of you. Thanks. But I need a shower, and . . . you didn't expect me," André stammered.

"You may as well stay," Maddy said. "You're here anyway."

André smiled at her. "I am here . . ."

They both laughed and went into the living room. Rocket stared after them and then looked over to his mom.

Risa picked up the bags. "Show André the shower and give him a towel. You can lend him a pair of shorts and a T-shirt. You have enough of them. They might be a tight fit, but we'll do a quick wash of his stuff and he can wear it home." She went into the kitchen.

"You need any help?" Maddy sang out.

"I'm good, dear," Risa said. "I'll tell you when to set the table."

"Tell Bryan. He's good at it," Maddy said.

Rocket went into the living room. Maddy was sitting down. He watched as she pulled the elastic from her ponytail and shook her hair out. Then she patted the sofa and André joined her.

"So what have you been doing this summer?" she asked.

"I've been working at a grocery store, doing the stocking," André said. "What about you?"

"I'll take the first shower, I guess," Rocket said.

"Not much. Hanging out mostly. I work for this juice place. It sells bubble tea, smoothies, juice — obviously — that kind of thing. It's only part-time, and they're always messing me up for hours. But I couldn't find a better job this summer, which sucks."

Rocket was getting that third-wheel vibe. "André, you want to change into something else for now?" he tried again.

"Is your job full-time?" Maddy asked André.

"Pretty much. It's unionized, so the pay's good. I got real lucky. My dad knows someone there, one of the owners," André said.

They were in their own world. Rocket gave up and went to take a shower.

He turned the water on. It usually took a minute or two to warm up. He thought about Connor and Raja. He couldn't let them intimidate him and throw him off his training. The puck dropped in seven days, and he needed to answer the call.

Then he thought about André. What price was too high to make the NHL? He'd never considered that. André had said Rocket should go for it because he had the talent. The truth was Rocket would pay any price because he had nothing else. Hockey was his only ticket out of this neighbourhood, for himself, for his mom and for Maddy.

He had to make the Axmen. If he didn't and had to try again next year, then the odds of getting to the NHL just got worse. His mom needed him to make it, to make money — NHL money. He wanted to get her out of this apartment more than anything. He'd buy her a big house and a car — everything she ever wanted. And Maddy needed to go to school. He knew she was already looking at colleges because they were cheaper. But she was so smart. If anyone should go to university, it was her. It was so unfair that rich kids never had to worry about these things.

Rocket tested the water. Still cold. He wondered when his life would get easier.

CHAPTER 3

Rocket took a big bite out of his sub.

"Ack. My shirt's been hit by sub sauce," he said.

"We could've eaten there like normal people," Maddy said.

"I can't sit. Too hyped. Besides, I can do this." He took a bite. "See, no sauce on the shirt this time."

"I'm very impressed."

They turned off the main street.

"This isn't meant to be a lecture," Maddy said, "but you could, maybe, spend some time with your mom tonight. You leave tomorrow, and I think she's a bit sad that you might be gone for the year."

"I think she's okay with it," Rocket said. "Axton's only a few hours away." He took another bite.

"Trust me on this one. You forget that you two are . . . you two have been together a lot since your parents separated, like you're a team. At least, that's how I see it."

"You'll still be here."

"I'm not her daughter."

He thought about what to say next. "I'm not saying

you are. It's just that I think of us as a family, the three of us, like we're in this together . . . like a family."

For a while they walked together quietly.

"That's a nice thing to say, and . . . that's how I feel, too." She let her sub fall into the bag, and she punched Rocket in the shoulder.

"Um . . . Ouch?" he said.

"Stop pretending to be so nice and brother-like, and go back to being the usual insensitive Bryan. You're going to make me cry," she said.

He rubbed his arm. "I thought you were supposed to be more mature than me."

"Shut up."

"Whatever."

A bottle suddenly skidded in front of Rocket's feet and smashed on the sidewalk.

"Where's your bodyguard, Peewee?" Connor called.

He and Raja ran across the street and stood in front of them.

"I don't want any trouble," Rocket said. "We're just going home."

Connor snatched Rocket's sub from his hands. "You ate my sandwich," he said. "Look, Raja, the dude actually ate my food."

"Total rudeness," Raja said.

"You can have it," Rocket said, "and I'm not interested in doing this."

He wasn't afraid of Connor. He'd dealt with way tougher guys on the ice. But Connor had Raja as backup — and Maddy had to get away from this.

Connor's mouth gaped open. "I'm sorry, what are you interested in?"

"I bet it's being a loser," Raja said.

Connor laughed, tossed Rocket's sub to the ground and kicked it aside. "So Peewee, do you care about what I'm interested in?"

"What are you interested in, Connor?" Raja said.

"I'm interested in kicking Peewee's butt into another century," Connor said.

"I have a phone and I'm calling the police," Maddy said.

Connor's head swivelled around. "You think we're going to let you make that call?"

"We don't need to make any calls," Rocket said. "We're just going home."

"You go where I tell you," Connor said.

Rocket knew he had to act now — show no fear. He charged into Connor with his shoulder and knocked him back. "Run, Maddy. Get out of here!" he yelled.

Raja threw a punch at Rocket's head from the side. It clipped him in the ear. Rocket took a step toward him, and Raja backed away.

"I'm breaking an extra bone for that," Connor growled, as he got up. His fists were clenched.

"Yeah, let's settle this," Raja said.

Maddy stood a few metres back.

"Get going," Rocket said to her.

She looked like a ghost, her face was so pale. She shook her head, moved next to Rocket and raised her fists.

"You don't think I'd hit a girl?" Connor grinned.

"I'm sure you're the type of guy who would," Maddy answered.

"Maddy," Rocket whispered urgently.

"Forget this. Grab her, and I'll take Peewee out," Connor said to Raja.

Connor threw a left jab at Rocket's face. Rocket blocked it with his forearm, and took a few steps back. Raja grabbed Maddy by the wrists.

"Let go!" she screamed. She kicked him in the shins.

"This girl is nuts," Raja said, letting go.

"Just keep her off me," Connor said. He faked another left jab and let loose a wild roundhouse. Rocket ducked under it and caught Connor in the ribcage with a wicked right hook. Connor grunted and stepped back, but only for a second. He came at Rocket with a series of jabs and a few right hooks. Rocket had no choice but to spin onto the street to keep his distance. Connor was much bigger, so Rocket had to make sure Connor didn't get him down. He also had to keep an eye on Maddy. So far she was holding her own. Raja was trying to grab her wrists again and she wasn't letting him. She also wasn't running away.

"Stand still, Peewee. Stop running around like a chicken," Connor said.

Maddy darted over and kicked him in the shin. "Leave us alone!"

Connor grabbed her arm and pulled his hand back.

"Let her go!" Rocket threw a right hook, connecting hard with the side of Connor's head.

Connor staggered back, his eyes darting wildly about.

Rocket shook with rage. "You're so tough? Let's do this already!"

"You've just made the biggest mistake in your life,

loser!" Connor said. Then he nodded at some people on the other side of the street. "We got company. This must be your lucky day. But this isn't over, believe me."

Rocket's right hand was throbbing. He could only pray it was over for now.

"C'mon," Connor said to Raja. "I think I saw a cop." He turned and disappeared down an alley.

Raja glared at Maddy and Rocket, his eyes bugging out, and then he followed Connor.

Rocket raised his gaze to the sky. This was bad. What if he got caught on the streets by himself when Connor was with the Brigade crew? Or worse, what if Maddy ran into them? He turned to her. Her eyes were red and puffy.

"I hate this place so much," she said. Her voice shook. "That Connor needs to go to jail. It's . . . it's . . ."

"Ridiculous," Rocket said.

She took a breath and opened her fists. "That'll do for now."

Rocket tried to make her feel better. "Connor thinks he's a big man," he said. "But he was too scared to fight André, and he just backed down from me. He won't bug us now."

"I'm not so sure about that," she said.

"Anyway, we'll probably be out of here soon. Mom's looking for a place closer to school."

They continued up the sidewalk.

"She won't be able to walk to work, then, and I'd feel bad if she moved just for me. And places by the school are a fortune."

Rocket had no answer. His mom had been looking

for a while, but everything was so expensive. He flexed the fingers of his right hand and winced.

"You okay?" Maddy said. "Is that the hand you hit him with?"

"Small price to pay for smacking that guy," Rocket said. "It hurts a bit."

"Hold on." She stopped and took his hand in hers. She pressed his knuckles. "Does this hurt?"

"Ow!" Rocket pulled his hand away.

Maddy's face clouded. "A little ice is probably all you need."

Rocket rubbed the inside of his palm with his left thumb. "It'll be fine."

They crossed over to their building and went in.

"I guess it'll be quality-time with Momsy tonight," Rocket said as they got in the elevator.

"Good."

"You can come out of your bedroom and hang with us for five minutes, as long as you don't talk, naturally."

"I have to be there the whole time," Maddy said. "You'll drive your mom insane with your boring hockey talk."

"Sorry. You said boring and hockey in the same sentence. That's not possible."

The elevator doors opened. There was a thick, stale smell of stewed beef in the hall that almost made him gag. The television was in 1207 was blaring. He really wished his mom could find another place. They went in.

"Hey, guys," Risa said. She was in the living room. "Did you enjoy your celebratory submarines?"

He would have enjoyed finishing his.

"They were great," he said. "Hey, Mom, do you feel like watching a movie or something tonight?"

"Are you packed for tomorrow morning?"

"Yeah, I think."

"Do you want to go over the checklist again?"

"I'm good."

"You have your toiletry bag, right? And toothpaste and a toothbrush and some dental floss? A book to read on the bus? What about all your hockey gear?"

"We went over it, Maddy and me. I'm good."

"You have to get up early enough to be at the bus station by nine o'clock," Risa said. "You won't have time to pack in the morning, so make sure—"

"What kind of movie do you want to watch?" he interrupted.

She sighed. "Okay, I admit it. I'm very sad about you leaving and I feel like crying. Sorry about bugging you so much."

"You're not," Rocket said. "Well, you are, but . . . I'm going to be sad a bit, too. It'll be weird, living with another family, going to a new school where I don't know anyone." He stopped suddenly. "I can't believe I said that. Totally jinxing it. I meant I won't make the team, so there's nothing to worry about. I'll be lucky to even survive the three-day training camp before getting cut."

"*Jinxing it*? I thought you were going to limit your superstitions to knocking on the front door three times before a game and wrapping the blade of your stick with ten strips of tape," Maddy said.

"You forgot about putting my elbow pads on before my shoulder pads, being the last one to leave the dressing room and crossing the centre dot with one skate during the warm-up," Rocket said. "Other than that, I'm letting the superstitions go."

That is, unless he said something about making the Axmen. Then he needed to take it back to cancel out the jinx.

"I'll make some popcorn," his mom said as she got up. "You guys choose the movie. Nothing too scary, please."

"Let's make it a girl night," Maddy said. "How does that sound?"

"I'm all for that," Risa said from the kitchen.

"It is sort of my last night here — for a few days anyway," he said. "Isn't that a bit cruel and unfair? You can't be that insensitive."

"Okay, but only because you're scared about Axton and you're probably going cry yourself to sleep tonight," Maddy said.

Rocket grinned. "You rock, sis."

"Obviously," she said.

Maddy turned on the laptop. "I have a good idea," she said. "I'll have it downloaded in a sec."

Rocket sat on the couch and leaned back. He wasn't going to cry himself to sleep, but he was scared. He wanted to make that team so bad it hurt. He'd been training himself to death the entire summer, when he wasn't working with Maddy at the juice bar. He couldn't be in better shape — or could he? His nerves were kicking up. It was hard to sit still.

"It'll be two minutes," Maddy announced.

"What are we watching?"

"It's a surprise," she said.

He threw a pillow at her.

"Such a boy," she said.

He'd miss his mom — and Maddy. If he made the team, he'd be billeted with a family in Axton until the season ended next spring. He was a bit scared about all the changes, but he was more scared that he'd be sent home. He had so much riding on this that it felt like there was a huge weight on his back.

Rocket rubbed his right hand. "I'm going to get some ice," he said.

"Is it bad?" Maddy asked.

He got up. "It'll be fine. I just have to ice it." He took a step and stopped. "Thanks, by the way. For back there. Those were some awesome fighting moves."

"No one messes with my bro." Maddy grinned.

Rocket held up his fists — and then groaned. His right hand was really hurting. He went to the kitchen and opened the freezer.

"Perfect," he said, pulling out a bag of frozen peas.

"What did you hurt now?" his mom asked.

"I banged my hand — running. I slipped on the sidewalk."

His mom came over. "Can I see it?

"It's fine," he said hurriedly.

She patted him on the arm. "I'm going to miss my little boy," she murmured.

"I'll miss you, too," he said.

She put her arms around him. He had a feeling she was crying a bit, and he had to blink a few times, too. They'd been through a lot together, the two of them. Like Maddy said, they were a team, and now it felt like the team might split up. He'd always be her son, of course, but things were different now. He wasn't a little boy anymore. She obviously knew that. He figured she needed him to be her little boy for one more night.

The popcorn began popping.

"I'm going to burn it," she said, rushing to the stove. "You can start the movie."

"We can wait," he said.

He went back to the couch and put the frozen peas on his hand. The cold stung his knuckles. A tight ball formed in his stomach. What if his hand was really hurt? Could he still grip his stick? This could be a disaster.

He pushed it from his mind. It was one punch. He could still wiggle his fingers. He'd be fine.

"You going to finish downloading that?" he said.

Maddy stuck her tongue out at him. "Already done."

Looking at her, the weight on his back felt even heavier. Maddy had to deal with Connor and the Brigade when he was gone. It almost made him feel sick to his stomach. He couldn't stay here and protect her, though. He had to go.

That gave him an idea.

"Hey, Mom," he called out.

She walked in with three bowls of popcorn.

"Maybe Maddy can come up to Axton for a day or two, for a little break before school starts? I could ask my billet once I get there." If Maddy disappeared from the neighbourhood for a few days, Connor might forget about things. And since Connor never went to school and Maddy got up early to go, she might be able to avoid him for months. There was after school to worry about, but Rocket couldn't think of a better plan right now.

"If she wants to, that's fine with me," Risa said.

"That might be fun. I'd be up for that," Maddy said.

"Consider it done," Rocket said. "Now roll the film."

Maddy attached the cord from the television to the computer and pressed the enter key.

Rocket felt grateful to Maddy for convincing him to hang out with his mom tonight. This could be the last time they were together like this — like a family — for a long time.

CHAPTER 4

Rocket's hockey sticks tumbled to the sidewalk. He kicked one and it spun around and whacked Maddy in the foot.

"Slashing penalty, goofball," Maddy said. "You've dropped them twice already. Did you dip your hands in butter?"

"Connor's rock-hard head. My hand is messed."

"Give them to me," she said, collecting the sticks. "Let's hurry. Your bus leaves in twenty minutes."

"Not my fault," he said. He gave his hockey bag a pull and they continued down the street. "Mom lost her mind. She was convinced I'd forgotten my nail clippers. I swear I had to actually show her they were in my kit bag."

Maddy adjusted the duffel bag strap across her shoulder. "You could have been a little nicer, Bryan. She was obviously upset, especially since she had to go to work this morning."

"I *was* nice to her. I watched that movie last night and talked to her and . . . I *need* to do this. I have no choice. She has to understand that. I'll make it up to her."

"Maybe a call tonight from Axton?"

"Don't you think she made me promise to Skype her about ten times already? It's not a big deal."

"I didn't say it was a big deal."

She'd been sniping at him all morning. He wondered if this didn't have something to do with Connor and Raja. "So, change of topic, but I was thinking a lot last night about the Brigade . . . I feel bad about leaving you."

She stopped and put the hockey sticks together in one hand. "Thanks, Bryan. But I'll be okay."

"I hate not being here to help out. That's why I thought it would be a good idea for you to come to Axton. Once school starts, you can avoid Connor easier."

"I figured as much."

"And I know I've been a bit of a jerk to my mom. She's worried about me going to a new place. But at least she won't need to spend any money on me. That should help a bit."

Maddy bounced the sticks lightly on the pavement. "This is important for you. This is what you've killed yourself for, all those games, the training. I get it. So I don't want you worrying about us. Think about hockey. We'll be fine."

"You want me to think about myself? I don't need help with that."

They both laughed.

"First things first. You've got to get that bus," she said.

They hurried into the terminal.

"Do you have the bus ticket?" Rocket said.

She stomped her foot. "Bryan! Your mom asked you before she left and you said . . ."

He couldn't hold the laughter in.

Maddy pressed her lips together. "You think you're so funny. Now I'm glad you're going."

"Don't throw a fit because I got you. Just be ashamed of yourself."

"Trust me. I am. Let's find that stupid bus so I can get rid of you."

They looked at the departures screen — bus to Axton, platform eighteen.

Suddenly Rocket heard a loud cheer and three kids came running over. The girl held a piece of Bristol board that read *Good Luck, Bryan* in big, blue bubble letters.

Rocket smiled at them in surprise. "Hey, guys," he said. He hadn't expected to see his old trivia teammates here. "Where are Des and Daniel? Did you kick them off the team?"

In grade seven, when things weren't going so well with hockey, Rocket had joined the trivia team as their sports expert. He'd been friends with them ever since.

"They aren't back in town until next week," Megan said. "This is all I could find on short notice. Hi, Maddy!" The two girls hugged.

Megan looked different. He hadn't seen her all summer. She'd been at her cottage and then working at a camp. Her lips were really red and her cheeks had a bit of colour to them. Her blue eyes seemed to be sparkling.

Megan was wearing makeup!

"Um . . . earth to Bryan," Megan said.

He'd been caught staring.

"Right. I'm good. Just a little spaced. It's been a crazy morning," Rocket said. He lowered his hockey bag to the floor. "Guys, this is nice. Thanks."

A tall, thin boy with very messy hair walked past Megan. "What's the capital of Madagascar?" he said.

"Bird, I'm the sports guy," Rocket paused. "But, it's Antananarivo. You want to take a shot, Nigel?" he said to the other boy.

"Largest city in Burundi?"

"Bujumbura."

"I can't believe you're leaving us," Bird said. "You're hitting your trivia prime."

"I've been focusing on geography. Tired of Nigel making me look bad."

"That's always been fun," Nigel said.

"You can still make me feel dumb in math, if that helps," Rocket said.

Nigel nodded. "Thanks. It does."

"I still can't believe you're ditching the school trivia team to play in the OHL. This is going to destroy your nerd cred," Bird said. "Just don't forget us when you're in the NHL making millions — free tickets and such."

"He gets free hockey gear in the OHL," Megan said. "That's a start."

"So, not so much with the millions right off the bat . . ." Bird said.

"The average NHL salary is a little over $2.5 million a year," Nigel put in.

"That would buy a sweet motherboard, a wicked processor and a totally awesome graphics card," Bird said.

"I guess we don't have to worry about our trivia team losing its nerd cred," Megan laughed.

Bird grinned and flashed two thumbs-up.

"The minimum salary in the NHL is $550,000," Nigel said, "so even if you kind of suck, all you have to do is make it."

"Bryan will make it," Megan said.

Easier said than done, Rocket thought.

A crack of thunder sounded.

"Who's in charge of this weather?" Bird asked. "The rain is going to totally mess my hair."

"I am, and I decided we needed some," Megan said.

"Why now, Evil Rain Princess?" Bird asked.

"To show you I'm all-powerful — and to clean your hair for once," Megan said. They all laughed.

"You should get to the platform now," Maddy said to Rocket. "You want to get a good seat. It's first come, first served."

"Okay," Rocket said. "Bye, guys. I don't know when I'll be back. It might be sooner rather than later. This is a tryout training camp for me, so I'll text when I know what's going on." He reached for his bag.

"I'll help you to the platform," Maddy said.

"We'll wait for you here," Megan said to Maddy. Then she turned to Rocket. "Take care, Bryan. I know you're going to do great. You'll make that team, totally dominate, and smoke guys and dangle defencemen and roof one for a top-shelf goal . . ."

Rocket hugged her and she held him tightly.

"Later, Bird, Nigel," Rocket said, letting go of Megan. "This is your year. In March, I'd better hear that you've won the trivia tourney." He pointed at them. "What city in Europe is known as the Pink City?"

"Toulouse, France," they answered.

"Unbeatable," Rocket declared, and he headed to the doors leading to the platforms.

"Go Rockwood Go! Go Rockwood Go!" his friends chanted.

He fist-pumped in rhythm and pushed the door open.

"Do you have anything to read for the bus ride?" Maddy said to him as he lined up.

This was an old joke of theirs.

"I forgot." He slapped his forehead. "So stupid. Now I'll have to listen to music and play games on my phone the whole way."

She snorted. "No wonder your brain is three-quarters mush."

"Three-quarters? I'm getting smarter," he said.

The line moved quickly. The driver threw Rocket's stuff into the storage hold.

"You'll do great. Just remember to *bring it*," Maddy said.

"Always. I'll talk to you tonight."

She gave him a hug.

"I'll ask my billet about you coming up. The exhibition season starts right after training camp. You may as well see a game." He winced. He had to stop jinxing himself.

"Sounds good."

"And tell me if there's a problem with Connor and Raja and the Brigade. Seriously. Tell me," he said.

She pointed to the door. "Get on the bus, Bryan."

"Passengers to Axton. Last call to Axton," the driver called out.

"Bye," Rocket said to her.

She was already heading back into the terminal.

He took a deep breath. *Bring it.* Ty, Adam and he had begun saying that when they were little kids.

Tomorrow he had to do exactly that.

He had to.

CHAPTER 5

Rocket shifted uneasily and leaned forward. His back was wet from sitting in the plastic chair. The bus ride hadn't been too bad, about three hours, but he'd been waiting for his billet for another hour. He hit *send* and waited for Maddy to text him back. His right hand hurt too much to text with, so he had to poke away with his left index finger.

Still waiting for Mr. Fabulous, he texted to Megan.

A man in a dark grey suit walked into the bus terminal, a Bluetooth receiver glowing in his ear.

"Got to go," the man said. "Let's keep talking. You know how high I am on Aaron. He's the complete package, and I think with the right representation and direction he can take it to the next level. You won't find a more dedicated agent than me. I travel all the time, so don't think I'm some hick from Axton. This is just where I want to raise my family." The man said goodbye and hung up.

His face grew grim as he tapped his earpiece. Then he pushed his glasses into place and squinted at the arrivals screen.

Rocket put his phone in his pocket and sat up straight. He had a bad feeling. The man's eyes settled on him.

"Bryan Rockwood?" the man said. His deep voice seemed loud in the small station.

Rocket stood. "Hi. I guess you're my billet?"

"You guess right. I'm Strohler. Carl Strohler." He looked Rocket up and down. "You're trying out for the Axmen? In the OHL? As in full contact and fighting against nineteen- and twenty-year-olds?"

Rocket took an instant dislike to him.

Strohler scratched the side of his face. "Fifteenth round, eh? Well, you never know." He nodded to the side doors. "I'm parked outside. C'mon." He tapped his earpiece. "Strohler. Talk to me." He walked off.

"Thanks for helping with the bags," Rocket muttered under his breath.

He slung his duffle bag across his back and reached for the handle of his hockey bag with his left hand. He looked at his sticks like they were a set of weights. His right hand was killing him. Suck it up, buttercup, he told himself. Trying hard not to show how much it hurt, Rocket picked up his sticks. He needed to find some ice, fast.

Strohler was already sitting in the driver's seat of a white SUV as Rocket got outside. The trunk was open. Rocket tossed his stuff in.

"I'm going to take a run to Chelsea tomorrow morning," Rocket heard Strohler say. He was still on his phone. "There's a kid there I like the looks of. He's playing Junior A this year, but he's a big kid, a winger — Nicolas Kingstone."

Rocket almost did a double-take. He'd gone to school with Kingstone for two years. When Kingstone had switched to another high school, Rocket had lost track of him. They hadn't gotten along very well. Kingstone liked to throw his weight around — probably because he had a lot of it. He'd been a big guy in grade seven.

Rocket opened the door to the back seat. A boy who looked about Rocket's age was sitting on the front bench. Beats headphones on, the music blasting, the boy kept his eyes glued to the phone in his hands. He was a big kid, kind of chubby, with curly brown hair. A woman turned around from the front seat and smiled. She looked tired, but her face was friendly and her eyes were sympathetic.

"I'm Kimberly Strohler," she said. "Sorry for being so late. We had . . . another appointment. We're really sorry. You must be tired after that trip." She looked at the boy. "Devin, honey. Can you scrunch over and let Bryan sit?"

Devin looked out the window, bobbing his head to the music.

"It's fine," Rocket said. "I'll take the back."

Her smile seemed forced. "Sorry about Devin. He can't hear anything with those things on."

Rocket sidestepped his way to the back seat. Strohler drove off.

"We'll be home in a few minutes. Axton isn't a big place compared to where you live," Kimberly said. "You can settle in, and then we'll eat. I've got you downstairs, so you'll have your own washroom."

"Awesome." Rocket said.

"We don't live too far from the rink, either," Kimberly said. "We can give you a lift most of the time. Otherwise, it's not more than a ten-minute walk."

"I can walk, no problem," Rocket said.

"I think Carl would live at the rink if he could," she said. She looked wistfully at her husband. "He wants to become a player agent — for hockey players."

Strohler tapped his earpiece. "I am a player agent," he said sharply.

"I thought you worked for Grandpa in his roofing company," Devin said.

Rocket wondered how Devin could suddenly hear.

"I'm focused on sports management now," Strohler said. "Pay attention and look up from that screen of yours once in a while. Or play a sport and stop being a geek."

Devin slumped in his seat.

"I've got a half-dozen awesome prospects," Strohler said. "I'll sign a few, and when one of them makes the NHL, I'll take five percent of everything. Couple of guys, and I'm making hundreds of thousands. Do the math. Roofing is for losers."

"Carl! My father has been very generous to us, and you've done well in the business," Kimberly said.

"You just watch. In five years, we'll be living large, and not in Axton — maybe in New York or Chicago or Toronto. I should've been playing pro in those cities," he said.

"I like it here," Kimberly murmured.

"That reminds me," Strohler said loudly. "It's Bryan, right?"

"Yes."

"There'll be a kid at camp named Aaron Cashman," Strohler said. "The kid's the real deal, and I'm totally close to signing him. I need you to be my eyes and ears on the inside. Get to know him, find out what he thinks about the coach, other agents, anything. Can you do that for me?"

"I guess," Rocket said.

"Everyone calls him Cash," Strohler went on, "which is kind of funny since he's going to make a ton of it. Kid's a stud — almost six feet already and a hundred seventy pounds, and he's only sixteen. Skates like mad and plays with an edge. You're a late-rounder. You'll never make his line, but you're both rookies, maybe use that to get close to him. You do this for me, and I can put in a good word for you with the coaches. They listen to me."

"Thanks."

Strohler tapped his earpiece. "Hey, how's it going? I have to dump my billet off at the house and we can meet. Yeah, at Victoria and Strachan. See you in ten."

The car turned a corner, continued on another hundred metres and then pulled into a driveway. It took all of Rocket's self-control not to burst out laughing. He could deal with Strohler if it meant living here. The house was huge! Bigger than Ty's and Adam's put together. It even had three garages. Roofing must pay very well.

Devin pulled his headphones off. "Are we eating right away?"

"Bryan just has to put his things away, then we can have lunch, honey," Kimberly said. "Can you wait?"

"Ya, I'm not hungry. I'll take a pass on it — maybe later," Devin said.

"You have to eat something," she said.

"Hey guys, I wasn't kidding," Strohler said. "I got to meet someone. Move it."

"We're going to eat soon," Kimberly said.

"I won't be long. Go ahead," he said.

"Can you just show Bryan around?" she asked.

He groaned and pointed to the house. "You see that? That's the house, Bryan. You'll be staying inside. Look around and you'll figure things out." He turned to her. "How's that for a tour? Now, c'mon. I got to meet Derek."

"All right," she said slowly. She opened her door and got out.

"Devin, don't forget to run those stats for me. I sent you an email," Strohler said.

Rocket could feel the chill in the air. This was totally uncomfortable.

Devin's headphones were back on. Kimberly's face was tightly drawn. She went to the trunk and took hold of Rocket's duffel bag.

"I can do it," Rocket said.

Kimberly slung it over her shoulder. "You can take your hockey bag. I have this."

Rocket slipped the sticks into the crook of his right arm and dragged his hockey bag with his left. He didn't want Strohler to find out about his hand. He probably knew Gold, and the last thing Rocket wanted was an excuse to be cut. Strohler reversed out of the driveway.

Devin stood at the door, hunched over, leaning against the wall.

"Are you not feeling well?" his mom asked.

Devin looked at her with half-opened eyes. She

pulled keys from her purse and opened the door. Devin went in quickly, kicked off his shoes and disappeared up the staircase and down a hallway.

Kimberly's eyes narrowed. "I'll show you how to work the garage door opener in a second. You can keep your equipment in there. Let me show you your room."

He followed her down a wide, sweeping circular staircase into a large room. At the far end, by the windows that overlooked the backyard, there was a beautiful pool table, a green light fixture hanging over it. To the right there was a Ping-Pong table, and at the other side there was a massive television and a wraparound couch.

Rocket used to think Ty had the most awesome basement. His wasn't even close.

Then it got better.

"There's a workout room," Kimberly said, pointing left. "It has a bike and weights. The sauna is in there, too, and a steam room. The dials are on the outside. Takes about ten minutes to warm up."

"Wow, thanks," he said.

"I want you to enjoy yourself," she said. "It must be hard to leave home at sixteen. How are you feeling, Bryan?"

Apart from his hand, he was feeling pretty good: workout room, sauna, steam room — it was like a hotel! "I'm not sure. This is what I've always wanted — to play in the OHL. I guess I just want to get going. Maybe I'm a bit nervous. I wasn't a high pick, so . . ."

"So you have to give 110 percent?" she said.

Rocket laughed.

"I don't know much about hockey," Kimberly said,

laughing, too. "Devin only played one year. He doesn't like sports that much. I'm learning, though." She paused for a moment. "Anyway, feel free to use the pool, too. You can go out to it through the door in the workout room, and there's a hot tub connected to it. Devin will show you how it works."

This place was unreal.

"That's the movie room," she said, pointing to two doors. "Devin plays his video games there. He can show you that, too. Over here we have the guest bedrooms, and this is the bathroom." She directed him down a long hallway. "You can choose whichever bedroom you like. If you need anything, let me know. I'm going to get lunch ready."

"This is amazing, thanks," Rocket said. "It's a beautiful house."

"I had fun building it," she said, with obvious pride. "I'll call you up when I'm ready. Just give me a few minutes."

She set off up the stairs.

"Excuse me, Kimberly," he said, following her. "But is there any chance I could get some ice? I just have a bruise I need to deal with — life of a hockey player."

"Of course. Are you sure it's not more than that?"

"Yeah, it's nothing."

"I'll get you an icepack." She continued up the stairs and then stopped. "Oh, and the password for the Wi-Fi is 'money,' with three dollar signs after it. We have unlimited service, so don't feel bad about using it."

"Okay. Thanks."

There were three guest bedrooms, which made him

shake his head. When they had a guest at his apartment, he had to sleep on the floor. Rocket dragged his duffel bag into the room closest to the bathroom.

Got here. No problems, he texted his mom, Maddy and Megan.

He lay on his bed and looked up at the ceiling. There was a bitter taste in his mouth, and all of a sudden his stomach felt full, almost bad enough to be sick. He sat up. His back hurt and his neck muscles were tight. What was wrong with him — other than the fact that if he messed up tomorrow he'd be gone, his life would be over and he'd have let down his mom, Maddy and all his friends?

Rocket decided to do some research on Axton's new superstar, Aaron Cashman. It would be better than losing his mind worrying about the tryouts. He opened up his laptop, did a search and came up with a ton of hits.

"You've got your own YouTube channel, Mr. Cashman," Rocket said aloud.

He clicked on the first video.

CHAPTER 6

Rocket paused at the arena door and waved to Kimberly in her car. Strohler had left early, so she'd been nice enough to drive Rocket over. She drove off and he went in.

Gold was set up behind a table. Rocket rolled his hockey bag over. He felt his sticks slipping from his arm. His right hand still ached, and he had no idea how he was going to play. He just knew he had to.

"Can I help you?" Gold said, staring at Rocket.

"I'm Bryan Rockwood . . ."

Gold smirked and flashed a finger gun at him. "I got ya. No prob. We're cool. How are things with the . . ." he looked down at his iPad, ". . . with the Strohlers?"

"Great, thanks. Carl says hi."

Gold gave him an odd look. "Okay . . . Well, here's a binder with the schedule. Don't lose it. This is your hockey bible. It's got all the drills, plays, schedules — everything you'll need. You lose that, you're toast. Okay?"

Rocket nodded.

"First thing, go down that hall to the second door

for your physical. Some guys are there already. After, head to room two and suit up for a scrimmage. Okay?"

"I guess."

Gold looked up at him. "Let me give you your first hockey lesson — from a guy who played in the NHL. This is Axmen hockey, and we run an NHL-style camp. There's no 'I guess' here. There's 'yes, sir' and that's it."

"Yes, sir," Rocket said.

Gold sat back in his chair. "I remember you now. I've been told you can put the puck in the net. Is that right?"

"I gue—" Rocket caught himself. "Yes, sir. I hope so."

"Hmm. Time will tell, I suppose. Toss your bag against that wall and get your butt to the exam room." Gold looked over Rocket's shoulder. "Bossy, what's up, bro? Loving the hipster beard on ya."

A large, older boy was strolling toward them. Rocket noticed the size of his hands — the two sticks he carried looked like toothpicks. He was easily over six feet tall, with broad shoulders and thick legs.

"Are you ready to rumble?" Gold said.

Rocket headed to the exam room. Bossy . . . that had to be Michael Boss. He was an overage junior, which meant he was twenty. He was also the team's tough guy — over two hundred penalty minutes last year.

Rocket went to the exam room. Two boys rode stationary bikes. They had masks over their mouths and tubes running from the masks to a machine. A young woman in an Axmen hoodie pressed keys on a computer. Her name tag read Stacy Chen. A man in a white coat, a stethoscope around his neck, was taking a blood pressure cuff off a guy seated on a metal stool.

Rocket recognized him instantly — Aaron Cashman. He was taller than he looked on the ice and slim, with very fair skin and light hair. Rocket slipped in, self-conscious, even though no one paid him the slightest attention.

"Will I live, Doc?" Cashman said.

"At least for today," the doctor said drily. "Can you give me ten deep squats?"

"I'll give ya the squats, but I can't be responsible for any sounds that come out," Cashman said.

The boys on the bikes snickered. The doctor took a deep breath.

The door behind Rocket opened and two guys walked in.

"How's it going?" the first guy said to Rocket.

He was big but not as thickset as Bossy, and he looked younger.

"This your first camp?" he asked.

Rocket nodded.

"I'm Kyle, and this is Nathan."

Nathan was shorter than Kyle, and stockier. He held out his hand. Rocket really didn't want to take it — Nathan looked like he'd have a strong grip. But Rocket introduced himself, then clenched his teeth and shook Nathan's hand.

"Get much skating in this summer?" Kyle asked.

He seemed like a friendly guy.

"Not as much as I'd like," Rocket said. "There's a rink around the corner from me; sometimes the manager would let me get on the ice before the hockey camps started in the morning."

Kyle elbowed Nathan. "I like this cat," he said. "Early morning skates show dedication. We put in a couple hours a day, plus gym time. We decided to go for it. We've been in Junior A for two years. If we're going to make it to the O, it's got to be this year."

"Were you drafted last year?" Rocket said.

Nathan let out a snort. "We weren't drafted any year."

Kyle answered the obvious question. "We're free agents. We live here and Nathan's dad knows Coach Alvo. He invited us." He held his arms out. "So here we are."

"You're done, Hoffer," the girl said to one of the guys on the bike.

The guy took his mask off. "Chenny, am I an awesome physical specimen, or what?"

"You're a specimen. I'm just not sure it's human," Chen said.

The other boy and Cashman laughed.

"I know Gruny's a gorilla," Hoffer said, pointing to the other boy.

Gruny couldn't really talk with his mask on. He rolled his eyes and kept pedalling.

Hockey nicknames were usually obvious. Hoffer? Had to be Kevin Hoffman. Gruny? David Grunfeld. They seemed to be the most likely linemates for Cashman. Both were third years and this was their draft year.

"Next," the doctor said.

"Go for it, bro," Kyle said to Rocket, who stepped forward.

The doctor raised an eyebrow.

"I guess players come in all shapes and sizes," he said.

Rocket grunted and sat on the stool. The doctor began to take his blood pressure.

"Take the shirt off," Chen said to Cashman. She held two sensors.

"Gee, Chenny, I hardly know you." Cashman grinned.

She slapped the sensors on his chest. "Hockey players are so funny. You should show some respect for your trainer."

"Chenny's in love with me," Hoffer said. "Don't waste your time, Cash."

"She hasn't met me yet," Cash said. "So what did these two losers get?"

"It's not a contest," Chen said. She poked some keys on the keyboard. "We're measuring how your body reacts to stress, as a benchmark. We can track improvement over the year."

"My coach used to say, 'If you ain't dying, you ain't trying,'" Cash said.

"Gruny's coach used to say, 'Gruny, get off the ice, you useless waste of space,'" Hoffer said.

Cash laughed.

The doctor listened to Rocket's heart, looked in his mouth and felt the glands around his neck.

"Give me ten squats, please."

Rocket counted them out and then stood behind Cash at the bikes. The doctor nodded at Kyle.

Chen sighed, clicking the mouse. "It's not working again. You can stop," she said to Gruny. "I have to reboot the computer."

Cash got up on a bike. Rocket figured he should strike up a conversation. Strohler would be happy.

"Did you play this summer?" Rocket said.

Cash shrugged. "I played four-on-four with some guys from my midget team, and I also had power-skating practices and strength training in the gym." He patted his stomach and grinned at Chen. "Got to get the six-pack ready for the ladies."

Cash was pretty well-built for sixteen. He'd obviously done a ton of training for this — professional training Rocket could never afford. Could running with André and training on his own really compare? The other guys were in serious shape, too. Had they all done power skating and strength training this summer?

"Worst part of the summer was the agents buzzing around telling me why they're so awesome. Before that, it was the coaches and scouts. I couldn't get a bag of chips without some reporter snapping a pic," Cash said.

"It'll get worse," Gruny said. "Reporters ask the most brain-dead questions: how'd it feel to get the win; what did you think after you scored; what did your coach say when you gave up the first goal? Trust me, you'll want to ram them through the boards to shut them up."

"Last year, after this game against the Steelheads, a reporter asks Gruny how it felt to get a hat trick," Hoffer said. "Gruny lets the dude hang for a good ten seconds, and then he says, 'It felt like scoring three goals in one game.'"

"And Hoffer says, 'It felt like watching him score three goals,'" Gruny adds.

The guys laughed. Rocket didn't think it was that

55

funny — more like rude — but he laughed so he wouldn't stick out. Cash laughed the loudest, and he high-fived Hoffer and Gruny.

Kyle joined Rocket.

"This is so frustrating. It's not working," Chen said. "There's a bug in the software. I can't record anything. Let me measure you boys, and we can do this later." She looked at her iPad. "Hoffer, you first."

"Good call. Check out the goods, boys," Hoffer said.

Chen measured his body fat with a skin caliper.

"Tell the fat pig to lose some weight," Cash said.

"Yeah, right," Hoffer said. He stepped on the scale and flexed his arms like a body builder. "This is 195 pounds of steel, baby."

"Stand against the wall," she ordered him.

He backed up. Rocket looked at the tape measure. Hoffer was a little over five ten.

Chen wiggled her finger at Gruny. He stepped forward and saluted.

"Grunfeld reporting for duty and ready to make Hoffer look like a little boy," Gruny said.

He had a solid frame. Rocket didn't look forward to battling him for the puck in the corners.

Coach Sonia had spent the last couple years teaching Rocket how to play against bigger players. He could only hope the lessons paid off.

Gruny stepped off the scale. "That's two hundred fifteen pounds, munchkins," he said. "Go get your ballet slippers."

"Lose ten pounds and you'll skate faster," Hoffer said.

"Why are you always behind me, then?" Gruny said.

Cash stepped up on the scale. "I'm pathetic," he moaned. "Only a hundred seventy pounds. Get me a milkshake. I got to bulk up."

"Don't worry," Chen said. "You're six feet already. I bet you'll hit six three easy and add at least thirty pounds by the time you're twenty."

Rocket stepped to the side. He didn't need an audience when they measured him.

"Go ahead," he said to Kyle.

Kyle laughed. "You're next, bro. No worries."

"Come on," the trainer said to Rocket.

Rocket found it hard to swallow. She measured his body fat.

"You certainly don't have to lose weight," she joked.

Rocket watched the lights flicker on the scale. The number flashed — 148. Hoffer and Gruny were snickering. Cash laughed outright.

"I like this guy. Makes me feel like a heavyweight," Cash said.

"I'm bigger than I look," Rocket said to make a joke of it.

Not his best comeback ever. Unfortunately, he had a feeling the worst was yet to come. He leaned against the wall, ever so slightly lifted his heels off the floor and stretched his neck as high as he could.

"We'll call it . . ." she pressed a ruler down on his head.

"I think it's six foot four," Cash said.

"More like . . . five foot six." She entered it on her iPad.

"I know who to call if anyone gives me a hard time on the ice," Cash said.

Rocket was done with the joke. He didn't respond.

"Let's get to the dressing room, boys," Hoffer said. "I got to show you the sweet skates the Nike rep gave me."

"Gold sent me two new pairs to break in over the summer," Cash said. "It's like you're not wearing anything, they're so light."

"You should check out my new stick," Gruny said. "Easton sent me, like, a dozen new ones to try out."

"I signed a deal with Reebok," Cash said. "I got to use their sticks."

The three of them left. Rocket waited for Kyle and Nathan to be measured, and together they walked out.

Kyle grinned at Rocket. "Who'd you sign your stick deal with?"

"I'm still comparing offers," Rocket laughed.

"Same with me," Kyle said. "And if one more person tries to give me free skates, I'm going to scream."

"It's not that funny," Nathan said. "Gold is sending Cash free skates, and he doesn't even know my name. How many free agents make it in this league, anyway?"

Kyle put a hand on Nathan's shoulder. "Not that many, but it's not zero. Come on, this is training camp. The OHL — the Axmen. We're here. Let's enjoy it."

"I'd enjoy it if it were a fair tryout," Nathan fumed. "Cash is on the team automatically."

"He was a first-round pick," Rocket said.

Nathan made a sour face. "Why didn't you tell me to be a first-rounder?" he said to Kyle.

Rocket liked these two. Things were tough for

them, but they hadn't lost their sense of humour.

"You guys know who the enforcer is on this team?" Rocket said, keeping the mood light. "I got to establish myself. Figure I'll drop the gloves early."

Kyle slapped Rocket on the back. "You got the right attitude, bro. And we don't need free skates and sticks. We have our own."

Nathan laughed. "And if we break our sticks we can borrow some from Gruny or Cash."

"What room are you in?" Kyle asked Rocket.

"Number two."

"We're in one," Kyle said. He held out a hand.

Rocket needed to stop shaking hands. He gave Kyle's hand a light slap, as if he were being cool.

"Good luck, guys. Bring it," Rocket said.

They went into their dressing room. Rocket stood in front of his door. He'd been totally stressed this morning. Now the stress was in overdrive. The coaches were probably looking to make cuts quickly if they were having a scrimmage in the first practice. It was going to be hard to play with his hand the way it was. The physical exam hadn't helped him relax, either.

You can't measure the size of a player's heart. He'd heard that stupid cliché more than once. The problem was that you *could* measure height and weight, and for the people making the cuts, size counted for a lot.

CHAPTER 7

The hockey bags told the story. Rocket counted seven returning players from last year. He figured they'd split the veterans evenly, so there were probably another seven in the other room. OHL teams were allowed to carry twenty-five players on their active roster, which included two goalies. They could also carry twenty-five reserve players, who could be brought up for a maximum of ten games. But the taxi squad wasn't Rocket's goal.

He knew the Axmen's goalie, Robert Glass, was back, so they probably needed ten new skaters and one goalie this year.

"Totally loving the scrimmage idea," Cash said to Hoffer. "I figured we'd be doing figure eights and suicides for three days."

"Gold did this last year, too," Hoffer said. "It's like a war out there. Guys are super-hyped."

"Ya, like that walk-on guy who tried to take my head off to get Gold's attention," Gruny said.

"Day one is full of meatheads," Hoffer said to Cash. "Be careful. Guys will be looking to take a piece out of you."

Cash seemed unimpressed. "Let 'em try. I can take care of myself."

The door opened. Gold, Alvo and Washington walked in. Rocket had spoken to Washington a few times during the summer, but hadn't seen Alvo since the draft.

Washington had called Alvo legendary, and Rocket knew Alvo had coached in the OHL for about twenty years. He had a rep for being tough — and having high-scoring teams. He'd also won three Memorial Cups, the last one four years ago.

"Listen up, boys. Coach Alvo wants a word," Gold said.

Alvo's cold, unsmiling eyes surveyed the room. Everyone quieted.

"I want to welcome you all to the Axmen training camp," Alvo began. His voice was low and gravelly. "I won't sugar-coat this. Every position is open. Every spot is up for grabs. I don't care who you are. You're here because we believe in you. Who stays depends on who wants it the most. We need to see who thrives under pressure, in real game situations, and that's why we're having three scrimmages over the next three days. We want you to have the chance to show us what you've got. So good luck to all of you. Coach Washington will be coaching the Red side. Mr. Gold will read out the lineups."

Alvo left as abruptly as he'd entered.

Gold tapped the screen of his iPad. Rocket leaned forward.

"This scrimmage we've picked four lines and three sets of D for each team, with a few spares. Not everyone will get to play. We'll do our best to rotate guys in tomorrow. You boys will be on Red. First line, we'll go with Cash at centre, Hoffer on the left and Gruny on the right. You boys ready to take it into another gear?"

Cash nodded and grinned.

"Beauty. Second line we'll have Bourquey in the middle . . ."

Rocket's heart was pounding through his chest. Would they put him on the wing or on defence — or on the bench?

"Third line will be Rockwood at centre, Bossy on the left and Fryer on the right."

Rocket pretended to fuss with his laces so the guys wouldn't see how relieved he was. Good sign that they'd put him at centre. Bourque played last year — this was his NHL draft year. Despite what Alvo said, Rocket figured Cash was a lock. That left two centre spots. Fryer had to be Hunter Fry. He was second year. Rocket didn't know a ton about him, other than he had a fair number of penalty minutes — although not as much as Bossy. He wasn't a scorer, in other words.

It would be strange playing with the team's tough guys. Rocket was used to being on the scoring line.

After Gold had rhymed off the rest of the lines, he said, "Plenty of physical play, please. We want to see some banging. Play hard. Play mean. I'll be watching." He slapped Washington on the back. "Good luck out there," he said and left.

"Get yourselves ready to play," Washington said. "I know you guys haven't been on the ice together before, so I'm not going to load you up with plays. We want an up-tempo pace and lots of back pressure, and Coach Alvo wants guys willing to play in all three zones. Glassy, how about you lead us out?"

The goalie waddled to the stick rack, pulled out his paddle and headed to the door. Rocket grabbed some tape from his bag. His dumb superstition of being the last guy out of the change room could be awkward. Technically, this wasn't a game, but he wasn't about to tempt fate now. He pulled a couple more strips around his shin pads as the rest of the guys filed out.

"Hey, Bossy, Fryer, come meet your new centre," Washington said as the two boys were about to leave.

Rocket tossed his tape in his bag and jumped to his skates. Bossy and Fryer looked over.

"Coach Alvo wanted you three together," Washington said. "I think you'll make a good unit. Rocket's playmaking will give you guys a chance to show off your offensive game a bit more this year. His nickname tells the story; he's all over the ice."

Bossy looked down at Rocket and half-smiled. "Yeah, cool," he said.

"Sounds good," Fryer said flatly.

"Have a good game, boys," Washington said. He held the door open. Bossy and Fryer walked out.

"You'll do fine," Washington said to Rocket. "Play your game and don't be intimidated. The boys are going to be a bit standoffish. They'll come around."

"Thanks, Coach. I feel good."

Washington tugged on Rocket's sweater. "Those boys aren't exactly afraid to drop their gloves. If you need help out there, just ask them."

"Okay. I will."

He slapped Rocket's shoulder pads. "You'll do great. Go for it."

Rocket had hoped to tape up his hand for support, but he didn't want to do it front of the coach or the other guys. It would raise too many questions. He hustled out to the ice. Washington was obviously looking out for him. He was less happy that the coaches thought he needed special protection. That wasn't good. He'd have to prove to everyone that he wasn't afraid of contact.

Most players were circling the ice in twos and threes. Two players were warming up the goalies. Rocket fell in behind a pack of guys and began to stretch out his legs. An elbow jabbed into his back, and when Rocket turned around, Kyle and Nathan were grinning back. They were in blue. Rocket slapped their shin pads with his stick.

"Didn't you hear? Red sucks," Kyle said.

"I kind of think it goes with my eyes," Rocket said.

Nathan looked at him. "I kind of think it does."

They all laughed.

"So who'd they put you with?" Kyle said.

"I'm centring a line with Bossy and Fryer," Rocket said. "What about you guys?"

Kyle shrugged, and Nathan lowered his head and tapped the ice with his stick. They swerved around the net.

"Alvo said he'd try and work us in when he could," Kyle said. "We're free agents, so . . ." He tapped Rocket's shin pads. "Good luck out there. I'm going to go for a bit of a skate. Might be my last chance."

He set off, Nathan right behind. Rocket was

impressed. Kyle could really motor. Nathan was a bit more awkward, with a jerky, loping stride.

Rocket spotted a puck against the boards and snagged it with his forehand. Stickhandling wasn't too bad. His bottom hand did most of the work. It hurt, but he could tough it out.

On a whim, he lowered his hands and tipped the puck onto this blade. As he passed the net, he stuffed the puck under the crossbar. He winced. That hurt — but this was the time to get some attention. Hopefully, Gold and Alvo noticed.

Rocket spotted another puck against the boards near centre. He reached out. A red sweater brushed past him and took the puck away, two other Red players close behind. It was Cash, and the chasers were Hoffer and Gruny. Cash pulled ahead and headed in on goal.

"Clear the way," Cash shouted.

The player warming up the goalie stepped aside. The goalie came out to challenge. Cash dipped his shoulder near the slot, and the goalie lowered into his crouch. Cash cut to his backhand, brought it back forehand and drove for the post. The goalie dropped into a butterfly and jammed his skate against the post, dropping his paddle on the ice to protect the five-hole. Cash whipped the puck across his body, let go of his bottom hand and, with one hand on the stick, tucked the puck into the corner of the net.

Cash raised his arms in the air. Hoffer pretended to bodycheck him into the boards. Rocket put his stick across his knees and glided across the blue line. He had a feeling Gold and Alvo saw that.

The buzzer rang out. The scrimmage was about to

begin. Rocket set off at top speed along the boards for a final skate. This was it.

"Get to your benches," a referee called out.

Rocket cut across the ice to Red's bench. The other Red players were crowded around Washington.

"Give me Cash's line first," Washington said. He pointed at centre with his iPad. "Rainer and Big Z, you're on D. Rest of you on the bench. Bourquey's line is next."

Rocket waited for the others to go in, and then he took a place next to Bossy and Fryer near the middle of the bench. The referee blew his whistle. The centres lined up and the puck was dropped. Rocket figured he should get to know his new linemates.

"You guys want to dump and chase or try to cycle it?" he asked them.

Bossy seemed to find that funny. "Maybe you should try not to get yourself killed out there, little guy."

Rocket gripped his stick so tight he hurt his hand again.

"How old are you?" Fryer said.

"Old enough," Rocket said.

Bossy laughed outright.

Fryer leaned over. "We're veterans and about twice your size, so you might want to chill the attitude."

The hair on the back of Rocket's neck rose.

"I'd hate to find you taped up like a mummy after this scrimmage," Fryer added.

Rocket kept his eyes on the ice.

"Good boy," Fryer said. "Behave yourself."

Rocket had heard about the hazing that went on.

These two guys could hold him down easy. He pictured himself wrapped up in tape and left on the floor of the dressing room. He'd never live that down.

Cash had pulled the puck to Rainer, who one-timed it to Big Z. The defenceman snapped a pass to Gruny at the boards. Gruny fed Cash at centre, who sidestepped a winger and dumped it in deep for Hoffer.

Rocket took a sip of water. His throat had gone dry. He took a deep breath and sat up straight. These two lunkheads weren't going to intimidate him. Chill the attitude?

Not in this lifetime.

CHAPTER 8

Washington tapped him on the back. "Rockwood's line is up next. Let's be ready."

Hoffer smirked. "Rockhead would be a better name."

"Leave the little guy alone," Bossy chuckled.

"Oh, that's good," Hoffer said. "Little Guy suits him."

Bourque swerved over for a change. Rocket stood and put his skate against the edge of the bench. No point responding to that garbage. When Bourque got close, Rocket hopped the boards and raced to Blue's zone to forecheck. A defenceman had the puck behind the net. Blue had also taken the opportunity to change. Rocket veered to discourage a pass to the defenceman's partner in the right corner. The defenceman came around the other side of the net. He had his left winger open for an easy outlet. Rocket cut back to force the pass.

The defenceman brought the puck to his backhand and skated back to the middle, edging hard on his inside left skate. He wasn't going to pass. He didn't think Rocket could stop him.

Rocket adjusted his angle, accelerated, lowered his shoulder and thundered into the guy's chest. Already off balance, the defenceman fell. Rocket dug his skates into the ice, sending up a massive snow shower, and at the same time, he reached for the puck with his forehand. The goalie dropped into his crouch at the top of the crease. The left winger was behind Rocket, and the other defenceman was coming hard. Rocket didn't have much time.

He pushed off with his back skate. The goalie waited for him to make the first move. Rocket stickhandled twice, then brought the puck to his backhand, shortside. The goalie dropped to the ice and pressed against the post. Cash had shown off his A-move. Time for Rocket to show his. He whipped the puck to his forehand. The goalie threw his stick out to poke-check. That caused him to lower his glove — which was just what Rocket needed.

Rocket put on the brakes in front, slipped the puck to his backhand and roofed it, glove-side. The puck nicked the crossbar and went in. A shot of pain went up his right arm.

The next second he was flying over the goalie and found himself in the net with the puck. The defenceman he'd stolen the puck from had nailed him.

"You're so dead, it's not funny," the defenceman snarled.

"Did you kill me before I scored?" Rocket said.

The defenceman raised his chin. "Do you want to go?"

"Go where?"

A fight was the last thing he wanted. His hand was killing him. He could barely hold his stick.

Rocket got up very slowly.

Bossy skated up and pushed the defenceman aside. "Feisty work, Little Guy," he said. He rubbed the top of Rocket's head with his glove.

The defenceman gave Bossy a look and backed away.

Fryer tapped Rocket's shin pads. "Little Guy's got some jam. Not bad."

"Lucky goal," Rocket said. "Let's get a real one." He tapped their shin pads.

Bossy chuckled. "Sounds good. Let's get 'er done."

They skated to centre. The referee already had a puck. Rocket swung around and set up. With his bad hand, he really only had the reverse-grip option. He had no power on his forehand. Blue's centre came in aggressively, reverse grip also. He swung his left hand forward and threw his shoulder inside, sweeping his stick over the dot. His glove clipped Rocket's chin.

Rocket stood up. "Ref?"

"Line it up," the referee said to him.

"Should be out of the circle for that," Rocket muttered.

"Stuff it," Blue's centre said.

Rocket put his stick down. He figured the centre would try the move again. The whistle blew. Rocket relaxed his shoulders and bent his knees. The puck dropped. The centre's left hand shot forward — too late. Rocket had pushed the puck between the guy's skates. He tried to hold Rocket up by throwing out his hip, but he'd committed to the sweep. Rocket avoided the check easily and gained possession of the puck.

The defencemen hovered at the blue line, unsure how to play him. Rocket was surprised to see Bossy charging alongside him on the left. Either Bossy had anticipated the move, or he had unexpected speed. Rocket went at the right defenceman, dangling the puck on his forehand. The defenceman charged. Rocket girded himself for another shot of pain and shovelled the puck over the defender's outstretched stick to Bossy. The defenceman extended his arms, but Rocket spun to his right, his back brushing the defenceman's gloves. He'd avoided the crunching check.

Rocket hesitated so he wouldn't be offside. The left defenceman had gotten back, the same player who'd challenged Rocket to fight. Bossy roared in over the line. Rocket figured he'd try to take it outside, but then — to Rocket's total surprise — Bossy snapped a pass to him.

Rocket cut wide right to create space. Now it was a two-on-one. In tight, he had to make a quick decision. He turned sideways, head up. Then, carving hard with his front foot, he kept going toward the net, waiting for the defenceman to commit. He didn't want to shoot. He wasn't sure his hand was up for it. Unfortunately, it seemed the defenceman wanted to force a shot, because he stayed right in the middle.

Five metres out, Rocket resigned himself. The goalie was way out of the net, though — not much to shoot at. Rocket gritted his teeth, tried to grip his stick like normal and pulled the puck back on his forehand.

Suddenly, the defenceman threw himself to the ice, feet first, going for the block. The goalie was still in a deep stance. Just as quickly, Rocket snapped the puck over to Bossy, who was charging hard for the net. The puck just made it under the defender's sliding figure.

Rocket felt another shot of pain in his hand, but it

disappeared as he saw Bossy angle his blade and send the puck up and over the goalie's right pad — another goal! The defenceman slid past him.

Two goals in one shift. Gold and Alvo couldn't help but notice.

Fryer put an arm around Bossy's shoulder. "Awesome play, Boss-man," he said.

"Way to go hard to the net," Rocket said.

Bossy grinned. "Nice pass, Little Guy. Even I couldn't miss that."

Rocket turned back to centre. This Little Guy thing was bad. Bossy and Fryer were vets, and if they began to use it, all the guys would. Hockey players were like that, especially during a tryout. They liked to pile on.

"Switch it up," Washington called out.

Rocket lowered his head and went to the bench. He'd barely stretched his legs.

Cash stood next to the forwards' open door.

"Excuse me," Rocket said.

Cash leaned both arms on top of the boards.

"Ooookay," Rocket said. He walked behind Cash and shuffle-stepped his way to the middle of the bench.

Cash held out his hand and high-fived Bossy and Fryer as they came off.

"Nice wheels," Hoffer said.

Gruny punched Bossy's glove.

"I kept telling you guys I was wasted on the fourth line last year. I'm a goal scorer," Bossy said.

"You're just a waste, bro," Hoffer said.

Bossy laughed it off, and he and Fryer sat down together.

The whistle blew and the play started again.

Rocket watched Red's fourth-line centre, number 12. He never wanted a guy to do badly, but he certainly wasn't cheering for his competition. Blue's centre won the draw back to his left defence, and then he blocked number 12 from forechecking. The puck went cross ice, then back to Blue's centre, who carried it over the red line and dumped it in.

Rocket reached for a water bottle. He wasn't thirsty, not after such a short shift. Bossy and Fryer were ignoring him, though, and he felt awkward sitting there. At least he could look busy. He took a few sips and then sent a thin stream of water over the boards. Blue was cycling effectively in the far corner. Number 12 was trying to win the puck. Blue's centre was proving too much for him to handle. Blue got a few shots off and managed to regain possession each time.

"Yo, number 12, get off the ice," Cash yelled.

Rocket wondered how he expected that to happen with the puck in Red's end.

"Guy's been on for three minutes," Cash fumed, slamming the shaft of his stick against the top edge of the boards.

"Keep the lines rolling," a woman's voice rang out from the stands.

"This is garbage, Coach," a man added.

Rocket looked up. The man was tall, very thin, with a pale complexion. The woman was tall, too, heavily made up, with bright red lipstick and green eyeliner. Her hair was bright blond and puffy, curled to just below her ears.

Blue's left defenceman fired a shot from the point. Glassy kicked it into the corner. Blue's centre beat number 12 to the puck and the cycle started again.

"Change it up!" the woman shouted.

"Washy's feeling the heat from the royal couple," Bossy said quietly to Fryer.

Rocket noticed Washington's lips were tightly pressed together, his eyes fiery.

"What do you think of our new star?" Fryer said.

Bossy arched his back. "Haven't seen enough. He's got skills, obviously, and size. The guy can skate."

"Not sure Alvo will be able to handle the parents," Fryer said.

"He's supposed to lead us to the promised Memorial Cup land," Bossy said.

"Kid's only sixteen," Fryer said.

"Better not let Gold hear you," Bossy said. "He's already planning the parade."

They were talking about Cash. The couple in the stands had to be his parents.

On the ice, Red finally got control and broke out of its zone. The right winger carried it over the blue line. Blue was caught with three forwards deep. It was a three-on-two.

"Number 12, get off the ice this century!" Cash screamed.

Number 12 either ignored him or didn't hear. The three Red forwards pressed on. Cash looked up at the ceiling. The winger passed to number 12, who fumbled the puck a bit and then sent it on to his left winger. The left winger reared back for a slapshot, but the delay had let the right defenceman get his stick over and he deflected the puck into the netting.

Cash flung the door open and charged onto the ice.

Rocket noticed him say something to number 12 before continuing on to the faceoff.

The guy looked bewildered as he came off. "What was I supposed to do?" he asked Washington. "It was an odd-man rush."

"That was ridiculous, Washington," the man in the stands called. "Who's the first line?"

"Don't worry about it," Washington said to number 12.

Number 12 stepped past Rocket and sat down. Rocket felt bad for him — not the best shift.

"Good work defending," Rocket said to him. "They didn't really have a good chance." No point kicking a guy when he was down.

"I didn't get a good warm-up," number 12 said. "Legs felt dead out there."

Gold leaned over the glass from the stands. Washington went over, and Gold whispered something in his ear.

"Let's watch the length of our shifts," Washington said loudly. "Last shift was too long. Can't have that."

"Hear, hear," Cash's mom said.

"Puck's in our end, and then a three-on-two . . ." grumbled number 12.

Red's right defenceman had the puck at the point. Cash called for it in the corner. Instead of passing to him, the defenceman shot the puck at the net. Cash smashed his stick on the ice.

Gold obviously wanted Cash out there, and Bourque's line was next. Rocket stretched his legs out. It felt like he hadn't even played yet.

"Let's double-shift," Gold called out. "Get

aggressive. I want my coaches obsessed with winning, like me." He went and sat down next to Cash's parents.

Rocket looked over at Washington. The assistant coach had his eyes closed. He didn't look happy.

Rocket took another sip of water. This shift wasn't ending any time soon.

CHAPTER 9

Rocket zipped up his hockey bag. He was tired, but in a good way. In the end, the scrimmage had gone great. Despite Cash hogging a lot of ice time, Rocket and his linemates had connected for two more goals: Fryer from in close, Bossy off a one-timer from the top of the circle. Rocket had assisted on both.

After lunch they'd gone back on the ice for drills, and he'd done well — he was up among the leaders in the skating. The two-on-ones were a bit difficult with his hand. He passed as much as he could. On the break-away drills, he always deked. He'd scored his share today, so he was happy. But he also knew he couldn't keep that up all camp. Eventually, he was going to have to shoot.

He was going to ice his hand all night. It had to get better.

The other great thing was that Kyle and Nathan had finally got a chance to show their stuff this afternoon. Kyle was a good, all-around player, and Nathan had one of the wickedest shots Rocket had ever seen.

The chirping was getting irritating, though. The

vets were giving everyone a hard time, so Rocket knew not to take it personally. The bad news was that the Little Guy handle was beginning to stick, and for that reason Rocket had no desire to hang out after practice.

He rolled his bag to the stick rack and reached for the door.

"See ya later, Little Guy," Cash called out.

A few guys snickered.

Rocket froze, the door half open. If he didn't answer, he'd be Little Guy *and* a wuss.

"Better Little Guy than Big Mouth," Rocket said.

"Ooooooooohhhh," the boys sang.

Cash's eyes narrowed. "Like, you're joking, right? The midget is talking trash? You'd better hurry, Little Guy. The daycare kids are going down for their naps."

"Whatever," Rocket said.

He left. As soon as the door closed, a cold sweat came over his body. Had he done the right thing? Talking trash was part of hockey, and he was a rookie. So was Cash, though. Why did he have the right to chirp at guys?

Rocket headed slowly toward the lobby.

But Cash wasn't just a rookie. He was The Rookie, and Gold's favourite. Plus, Strohler seemed to expect Rocket to be Cash's buddy.

"Dumb, Bryan," he muttered to himself.

Strohler was talking to Cash's parents near the snack bar. He was out of luck if he thought Rocket was going to be Cash's new BFF.

Devin spotted him from the corner. He took off his headphones. "How was practice?" he said.

"Not bad, thanks. You been here long?"

Devin smiled weakly. "Dad wanted to check out his

prospects. He has his eye on a couple of them, like that Cashman. I was keeping stats on them, like their number of shots, how many times they scored."

"You watched the scrimmage?"

"And the drills. Dad really wants Cashman. He's over there with Cashman's parents, telling them how well he did. Like, his percentage on two-on-ones and stuff. His parents were watching, too, so I don't really get why I had to keep the stats."

"You must really love hockey to watch an entire day of training camp," Rocket said.

Devin shrugged, then looked over at Strohler. "Dad wants me to find out how you did with Cashman."

"You guys don't fool around," Rocket said. He stifled a laugh.

Devin was dead serious.

"My dad just wants to know what you talked about, how you're getting along and what Cashman is thinking, about agents and stuff. It's kind of important. It's sort of why you're living with us."

Rocket was a bit taken aback. The reason he was living with them? "Um . . . it was a busy first day — not a lot of time to talk, really."

Devin leaned forward. "You can't tell him that. He'll freak. Dad says you're our Trojan Horse. You're supposed to be our secret agent on the inside. Think of something. Make it up, even. But make it good."

He sounded worried.

Strohler was shaking hands with Cash's parents.

"Okay, Dawn, I'll speak with you tomorrow," he said to Cash's mom. "Chris, your boy looked real comfortable out there. Impressive."

"I thought the line changes were garbage," Chris said, his chin jutting out. He and Dawn left to speak to Gold.

Strohler beckoned Rocket and Devin over.

"Did you buddy up with Cash?" Strohler demanded.

Devin looked at Rocket.

"For sure. Yeah." Rocket paused. "He's a nice guy."

"Let's hurry," Strohler said. "I got a call in ten minutes. You can fill me in while we drive home. Devin, can you hustle for once in your life?"

Devin tapped his right hand on his thigh and jabbed the other in the air, head bobbing. Rocket was standing next to him. He didn't hear any music from the headphones. Strohler was already out the door.

"We should maybe hurry," Rocket said. "'Cause your dad . . ."

Devin tapped away to the music.

The trunk was open when Rocket got to the SUV. He tossed his bag and sticks in and sat in the back row.

"Could you be slower?" Strohler said to Devin as he got in.

"Bryan, what did you and Cash talk about?" Strohler asked, reversing out of the parking spot.

"Not much . . . Hockey stuff."

"Like?"

"I wasn't on his line, so I didn't really have—"

"You were on Red together," Strohler cut in. "Did he mention anything about an agent?"

"He said he didn't have one yet, but lots of them tried to get him to sign during the summer," Rocket offered. That much was true.

"Interesting. Did he give names?"

Devin was right. He wanted real information. Problem was, Rocket didn't have much.

"I said, did he give names?"

"He didn't mention anyone specifically, more like agents in general," Rocket said.

"Job one is to get me the names of any agents he's speaking to. That's critical. Can you do that?"

"I can try."

"Make it happen. I need to know the competition. What else?"

"He worked out a lot in the summer."

Strohler grimaced. "No kidding. I mean, what else about who he might sign with?"

"He has a stick deal with Reebok."

Strohler slapped the steering wheel. "I knew Chris was a liar. He's a skinny little weasel. Total snakes, the lot of them. 'Oh, we haven't signed any deals yet. We want to keep our options open,'" he mimicked in a high-pitched voice. "They're playing me."

The SUV burned through a stop sign.

"You got to try and hang with him more, buddy up to him, invite him over to our house. You can play video games. Find out his favourite game." Strohler was getting more and more excited as he spoke. "That's perfect. All boys love gaming. Tell him we've got a huge TV and a sweet game console and he can play whatever he wants. Invite the other guys on his line, too, Hoffer and Gruny. Get them all over. Then I'll come in, do my thing, get the connections, and I'm off to the races." He gave the steering wheel another whack and laughed.

The SUV raced around a corner. They went right, left and then whipped into the driveway. Rocket felt relieved they'd made it in one piece. The guy drove like maniac.

"Okay, my call's here. Get your stuff out of the back and toss it in the garage," Strohler said.

The garage door began to open.

Strohler touched his earpiece. "Gentlemen," he said. "How are we today?"

Rocket pulled his bag and sticks out as quietly as he could and put them in the garage.

"Didn't Carl pick you up?" Kimberly said as he walked into the house.

"He's in the car," Rocket said. "On a call."

Kimberly's eyes narrowed, but then she smiled at him. "How was your practice?"

"Good. Intense. Tomorrow will be tough. We have dry-land training and then a scrimmage."

"I imagine you're hungry. Dinner will be in an hour. Is that okay or would you like a snack?"

"I'm fine, thanks," Rocket said.

"Feel free to go for a swim. I turned the heat up a bit. I figured after such a hard day, you'd enjoy a little dip."

"That's really nice. Thanks. Maybe I will."

"Ask Devin if he wants to join you. He's been in the arena all day. He should get some fresh air."

Rocket headed down to his room. Kimberly seemed really nice. How'd she end up with someone like Strohler?

Passing the movie room, Rocket heard gunshots, so he opened the door. Devin was already playing World of Warcraft.

"Yo, Devin. I'm probably going to hit the pool. You want to come?"

It felt weird asking Devin to come for a swim. It was his pool.

Devin put the game on pause. "What really went on with Cashman?"

Rocket stepped into the room and closed the door. Something told him Devin could be trusted. He didn't seem very close to his dad. "I'm not sure I can actually do what your dad wants."

"You mean Cashman's not coming over to hang with me?" Devin said. The corners of his mouth moved up slightly. Rocket knew he'd been right. Devin got it.

"He's a huge jerk," Rocket said. "Acts like he's in the NHL already. He spent the day chirping at everyone. Especially me."

"Why you?"

Rocket leaned his arms on the top of a couch. "No idea. Maybe because I don't have a stick deal with Reebok."

"Really?"

"Well, maybe it's more that I'm five foot six, weigh a hundred forty-eight pounds and got drafted in the last round. I'm a good target or, more like, a good joke — a good, *little* joke."

Devin turned around in the chair to face him directly. "You got a goal and three assists in the scrimmage, and you had a seventy-four percent success rate at getting a shot on the two-on-ones." He shrugged. "I figured I may as well keep the stats on you since I was there. You're a good player — always around the puck and a good passer. Maybe you could shoot more. Your line had good puck possession — way higher percentage than Cashman's line. You have a good chance of getting on as the third centre, behind Cashman and Bourque, although it's still early."

"Wow, I'm impressed."

"My dad taught me. I do the stats at games, so he can watch the play."

"You go to many games?"

Devin lowered his brow and looked up at Rocket.

"I'll take that as a yes," Rocket said.

"I'll be honest with you. Your size is an issue. Gold likes his players big. My dad, too."

"Guess what my nickname is on the team?"

"What?"

"Little Guy — not exactly a hockey classic."

"I looked you up. Aren't you called the Rocket? That's kind of a hockey classic, isn't it?"

"Not sure Rocket is going to catch on. Little Guy seems to be driving ahead at the moment. Anyway, let's forget about hockey and hit the pool. Your mom said you could show me how the hot tub works."

Devin put the controller down. "A hot tub would be good for your muscles. They worked you hard today."

Rocket was beginning to like this guy. He was kind of a geek, but he was honest and had a sense of humour. And he knew his hockey — Rocket always liked that.

"Give me a sec and I'll throw on my suit," Rocket said. "And is there any chance you could find an icepack?"

"Are you hurt?"

Again, Rocket decided to trust him. "I banged my hand up a few days ago. It's bugging me."

"I assume that explains the lack of shots," Devin said.

"You got it. I'm going to have to fight through it. If guys figure out I can't shoot, then they'll play off me," Rocket said.

"The latest research suggests that after the first twenty-four hours, you are better off applying direct heat to the injured area," Devin said. "It's been found to be very beneficial. We have these beanbag heating bags. I could warm one up."

Rocket had never heard that before. Devin didn't sound like the type who was wrong too often, though. The ice certainly hadn't helped much.

"I'll try it. But Devin, can we keep this between us?"

"Sure."

Devin went off to get changed and get the heating bag. Rocket went to his bedroom and closed the door.

For a moment he felt exhausted. That was a lot of hockey today. But it wasn't his body that was tired. The mental stress was way harder than the physical stuff. He felt like a bug under a microscope: every move noticed, written down and analyzed. Even Devin had stats on him.

His laptop beeped. Maddy was Skyping. He looked at the time.

"Whoops," he said as he answered.

"Thanks for only being twenty minutes late. I've got to get going soon," she said.

"Sorry, practice went later than I thought."

"Whatever. I didn't want to talk to you anyway."

"Actually, I don't have a lot of time either. I have to take a hot tub — after I swim in the Strohlers' heated pool."

Maddy's head drooped. "You're joking, right?"

"I am a little. First I'm going to hit the sauna, or maybe the steam room, then go for the hot tub."

"Are you staying at a five-star hotel?"

"Almost. This place is insane. Nicest house I've ever seen. These guys are so loaded, it's crazy."

"Well, we have a new air-conditioning system here — someone smashed the window in the lobby door." She laughed.

Rocket slumped forward. "Are you serious? Who did it?" He didn't find it funny.

"Who knows? But anyone can walk in and the super-intendent doesn't care. Your mom is freaked out, though. Maybe I am, too. Anyway, I'm not sure it beats a pool."

"Sorry, Maddy."

"It's nothing. Not like this is the first time someone broke a window here."

"I know, but I feel bad for you." He paused. "I'm still taking the hot tub, though."

"I figured."

"You got to come up and stay for a night or two. They have tons of extra rooms. I even have my own bathroom, and it's two times — no, make that three times — bigger than ours. There's a tub and a shower and *two* sinks. Not sure why anyone would need two sinks. I use them both, though."

"Good to hear you're keeping yourself clean."

"Ha, ha. Maddy's being funny. Any trouble with Connor and his crew?"

"Nope. I haven't even seen them. I'm sure they're spreading their usual joy. Anyway, I have to go. There's someone at the door."

"Who is it?"

"Um, just a friend. We're going to a movie."

"Who is it?"

"Rocket!"

"Tell me," he said.

Maddy had gone red in the face. "Fine. It's André. He asked me to go to a movie tonight. I figured, why not? No big deal."

"I didn't say it was. Say hi for me." He grinned at her and wiggled his eyebrows a few times.

"Goodbye, Rockwood."

"See ya, sis."

Her face softened. "See ya, bro."

The screen went blank.

Maddy and André were going to a movie. That was cool. Why shouldn't they be friends?

Rocket went out to the pool and put his towel down on a lounge chair. On the other side of the deck there was a gazebo and, next to it, a big barbeque and a fridge. The deep end of the pool had an awesome diving board. It was built into a mountain of rocks and stones. This place really was insane.

He flexed the fingers of his right hand. He hoped Devin was right about the heat.

Devin came out and pressed a button. The hot tub began bubbling away. For the first time since Rocket had met him, Devin was actually smiling.

"You thinking swim or tub?" Devin said.

"No brainer," Rocket said. "Hot tub all the way."

CHAPTER 10

Rocket picked himself up from the gym floor. He shouldn't have done those push-ups. He'd tried not to put any pressure on his hand, but it was impossible not to. The hundred sit-ups had been fine. He was used to doing five hundred a night, so he'd been among the first to finish, along with Kyle and Nathan. He was less thrilled that Cash had finished at the same time.

Chen hopped to her feet. She'd been drilling them with exercises for half an hour, and lots of guys were fading.

"I'm not sure if you noticed the track around the field when you came in," she said, "but it's there, and it has your names on it. Head out that side door, please — and move it!"

She took off like a jackrabbit to the door, beating them outside. She'd done all the exercises with the team and was faster than any of them. The boys filed out. Gold and Washington were standing on the track.

"Give me a *Go Axmen Go!*" Chen yelled.

A few guys offered a weak cheer.

"That just earned you twenty push-ups," Gold said. "Next time make it count."

Rocket groaned inside. Not more push-ups. He pounded them out painfully.

"So how about it?" Chen said.

Rocket joined in a loud cheer this time.

"Much better," she said, clapping a few times. "Welcome to the ten-minute run, better known as the 'Run With Death.'" The veterans groaned. "Rules are simple. Run around the track as many times as you can in ten minutes — then fall to the ground and catch your breath."

"We're looking to see who can fight through the pain," Gold said. "If you're looking to impress us, now would be a good time."

"Hard at it, boys," Washington said.

Kyle held out his fist to Nathan. "You ready?"

"Let's go suffer," Nathan said, punching it.

Rocket really hoped these guys would get a chance to make the team.

"How many laps you figure we can do in ten minutes?" Kyle said to Rocket.

The track looked smaller than an official one.

"Anything over seven would be pretty good," he guessed.

"Line it up," Chen called. She formed a circle with her thumb and forefinger, brought it to her lips and, when everyone was at the start line, let out an astoundingly loud whistle.

The guys pressed forward like a wave, chugging up the straightaway in a pack.

"Let's make a move," Nathan said, as they entered the first turn.

"Wait," Kyle said.

The tempo remained high as they continued on to the second straightaway. Rocket settled into an even pace. His legs and shoulders were stiff from the earlier exercises, and he wanted to cruise through the first lap to loosen up. The pack was stretching out as they finished the third corner and headed back to the start line.

"You tired yet?" Kyle asked.

"You kidding?" Nathan said.

The pair shifted to the outside and motored up the straightaway.

"Run hard, boys," Chen yelled, clapping her hands.

Gold was tapping away furiously on his iPad. Washington looked like he was taking a video with his phone.

A few of the guys gave Kyle and Nathan a hard time as they pulled ahead.

"Check out the dynamic duo."

"Too bad you guys can't skate that fast."

"This is hockey, not cross-country."

Kyle and Nathan took no notice and soon were ten metres ahead. A small group of guys began to pull away with them, and Rocket kept up. He didn't want to lose touch with the front runners. Rocket had done his fair share of cross-country, and he ran almost daily to keep in shape. Gold had said this was a chance to impress, and Rocket wasn't about to miss out.

Over the next five laps, the gap between the leaders and the main pack grew larger and larger until the leaders were almost half a lap ahead. All the guys were hurting, Rocket included. Sweat stung his eyes, and his chest and legs were burning. Rocket forced himself to ignore the pain, and he pushed himself hard around the second corner. He passed a few more guys as they headed into the back straightaway.

"How much longer?" gasped Rainer, one of the defencemen.

"What lap are we on?" Glassy said.

"*Sept*," Bourque said.

"In English?"

"Seven."

Glassy moaned. "Longest ten minutes of my life."

"Sixty seconds to go!" Chen yelled, clapping away. "You guys are awesome — amazing!"

Rocket roused himself. He'd lost focus a bit after that last corner. Sixty seconds to impress. Kyle and Nathan were still out in front by three metres. He wondered if he could catch them.

"Good day, gentlemen."

Rocket heard a pair of shoes running up behind him.

"It's a great, great day for a run," Cash said in a Scottish accent.

He cruised past Rocket, Glassy, Bourque and Rainer.

"Forgot to mention I was state cross-country champ — five times," Cash laughed.

"Fancy-pants forward," Rainer managed.

Cash didn't let up until he'd passed Kyle and Nathan. Rocket gritted his teeth. Cash would win, and that's all the coaches would see — their superstar was also a track athlete.

Rocket urged his aching body onward. Metre by

metre he gained ground. Soon he grew level with Kyle and Nathan.

"Let's do this," Rocket said.

"Catch him, bro," Kyle said. "I'm done."

"Bring him down," Nathan said.

Rocket was still two metres back. The pain was almost unbearable, but not as painful as the sight of Cash's long, loping stride eating up the track. As Cash entered the corner, Rocket pulled even.

"Little Guy, I didn't know you had it in you," Cash said. "I'm almost impressed. You're not going to beat the Cash-Man, though." He ran ahead.

Rocket willed himself to keep up. "Wait for me," he panted.

Side by side they powered through the corner to the back straightaway. A group of stragglers were about 50 metres ahead. Rocket felt lightheaded, almost sick. These ten minutes felt like three days. The corner loomed.

Tweet!

A shrill whistle announced the end of the race. The runners up ahead staggered to a stop, hands on hips or knees. Cash didn't slow down.

"You're not going to beat me, Little Guy," Cash said.

"Ten minutes is over," Rocket said.

"Then quit."

Rocket desperately wanted to. But even more desperately, he wanted to win.

They came out of the corner in a dead heat.

"Make way," Cash shouted. "Grudge match."

"Go for it, boys," Hoffer said.

"Little Guy can run. Go figure," Gruny said.

Little Guy, Short Stuff Shrimp, Midget, Tiny Tim, Timbit, Peewee — the insults about his size were never-ending, and he'd been hearing them all his life. As his rage grew, his pain melted away. He was going to win.

Gold stepped onto the track and held his hand up.

"I'm the finish line. Go for it," he yelled.

Guys had crossed the infield to watch.

"Come on!"

"Push it!"

"All the way!"

Cash was breathing hard now, too.

Ten metres.

Rocket summoned every last ounce of strength. Pumping his hands, driving his leaden knees, he threw his chest out. Cash leaned his head forward. Gold threw his hand down.

"Cash wins it!" Gold cried.

Rocket veered off the track and went down to one knee. He was seeing stars.

"Awesome performance, bro," Kyle said. He draped his arm around Rocket's back.

"The Cash-Man cometh first — again," Cash said. He put his hands over his head.

"That's what I call leadership, Cash," Gold said. "That's the kind of compete level we want."

Gold held his fist out and Cash gave it a bump.

"Gather around me," Gold said.

Rocket's head pounded in rhythm with the beating of his chest. A centimetre — that was all he'd needed. If he hadn't gone out so slowly, if he'd pushed it in the middle of the race . . . It didn't matter. He'd lost.

"Did Cash actually win?" Nathan asked quietly.

Rocket took a deep breath. "I choked. I should've started out faster."

"That's not what I asked," Nathan said.

Rocket thought about it. "It doesn't matter now," he said.

"You did come second out of more than fifty guys," Kyle said.

"You and Nathan came third and fourth," Rocket said.

"Technically, *I* came third." Nathan grinned.

"Not bad," Chen said to the team. "A special shout-out to Cash for winning and . . ." She looked over to Washington.

"Bryan Rockwood," Washington said.

". . . and to Bryan for that death-sprint to the end — loved it. Now, listen up. Mr. Gold is going to explain what's happening next."

"Thanks, Chenny," Gold said. He poked at his iPad. "We'll take forty-five minutes to get back to the rink and shower up. Then go to room 107 for some video work with me and Coach Alvo. Lunch follows, and then it's a scrimmage. Lineups will be posted on the bulletin board in the lunchroom. Okay? Let's hustle back."

"Why don't we run back?" Chen said.

"'Cause we don't want to," Hoffer said.

She laughed. "A nice and easy jog to warm down. It's important to give the muscles a chance to relax, and the best way is exercise. Sounds crazy, but it works. That's why the pros ride stationary bikes after games."

She set off for the gate at the far end of the field.

Rocket fell in mechanically behind the pack. Kyle and Nathan ran beside him.

Not a word was spoken. Rocket knew they were all thinking about the same thing. Would Gold care who came second, third and fourth? Would he tell Alvo? Or would he only remember who won?

CHAPTER 11

Kyle nodded at the large platters on the table. "We're in the big leagues now, Nathan," he said. "Looks like tuna, turkey and . . . some sort of mystery sandwich. This is the good life."

"Then why can't the guys at the front grab one and move on?" Nathan grumbled.

Rocket looked on wistfully. "Remind me to run to the lunchroom tomorrow. Back of the line is a bad place to be at a hockey training camp."

"Front row for the video session put us behind the eight ball," Kyle said.

"Sorry," Rocket said.

He'd made them sit up close.

"No worries, bro," Kyle said. "Alvo's not the friendliest cat in the world, but he knows his hockey. Was that ten thousand things to remember when you break out of your zone?"

"He won't be the easiest coach to play for, but I respect anyone who can teach me about the game," Rocket said. "At this level, we have to think two or three passes ahead — in the pros, four or five."

"Hear that, Nate? We're going to be pros," Kyle said.

"Right now I'd settle for a mystery sandwich," Nathan said.

Rocket laughed. Nathan seemed glum and ultra-serious, but he came out with some wicked one-liners. Rocket peered around to the front of the line. Cash, Hoffer and Gruny were still checking out the choices.

"The whole point is to be an unrestricted free agent," Cash was saying. "I'm going to break in at eighteen, and when I'm twenty-five, I'm cashing in — pun intended. I go to the highest bidder."

"I don't know," Hoffer said. "You got to play for seven years to be a UFA, and by that time you're already earning millions. I'd rather win a Stanley Cup than play for a loser."

Cash picked up a sandwich and then put it down.

"I'm going to kill him," Nathan whispered.

"That tuna sandwich could be worth something one day," Kyle whispered back. "Actually touched by the one-and-only Aaron Cashman."

"The key is to get the first three years over with," Gruny said. "Then you test the waters as a restricted free agent."

"Restricted free agents almost never change teams," Hoffer said. "The team that signs them has to give up draft picks."

"Gruny's right," Cash said. "It's the threat that's important. You can take them to arbitration, too. The player always gets more — and then you kill it as a UFA."

"Your team might trade you," Hoffer said.

"A trade is okay. Shows you're wanted," Gruny argued.

"I'd trade you for a bucket of pucks and a tuque," Cash said to Hoffer.

"I'd trade all three of them for half a buttered bagel," Nathan said.

Rocket and Kyle chuckled.

"That's funny, is it?" Cash said, pointing a sandwich at them. "Like you guys are planning on becoming UFAs? Maybe in house league."

"Don't be so harsh," Hoffer said. "Maybe the East Coast League."

"Or the KHL in Russia," Gruny said. "They can earn ten rubles and a cold shower a month."

Kyle looked away. Nathan crossed his arms and did the same. Gold, Alvo and Washington walked into the lunchroom carrying trays with food and sat at a table. Gold waved at Cash, who, along with Hoffer and Gruny, went to sit with him. The line moved quickly after that.

"There's a free table over there," Rocket said to Kyle and Nathan.

"You guys stoked for the scrimmage?" he asked as they sat down.

"I want to be," Kyle said. "Not sure we're going to get a chance to play."

"Story of our lives," Nathan said. "Three seasons ago, I swear we had six coaches, and their sons were on for every power play. No wonder we didn't get drafted. We hardly got on the ice."

Rocket had been impressed with them yesterday during the drills. "You've obviously played a lot."

"Thank Nathan's dad," Kyle said. "He built a backyard rink — we've basically lived on it since we were five."

"I have three older brothers, so we had some legendary battles," Nathan said.

"We have outdoor rinks in the city. Me and my buds used to play on them after school," Rocket said. "Something awesome about playing outside — totally old school."

"Don't have to tell me, bro," Kyle said. "I was always Gordie Howe."

"I was Stan Mikita," Nathan said.

"I'd have been Joe Primeau."

"Whoa, where'd you come up with him?" Kyle asked.

"Toronto Maple Leafs, the thirties. He was part of the famous Kid Line, with Charlie Conacher and Harvey 'Busher' Jackson. All three are Hall of Famers," Rocket said.

Gold signalled for everyone's attention. "You boys enjoy the video session?" he said.

Cash and the others nodded, but Rocket wished Alvo had done the entire thing. Gold had talked a lot — and hadn't always made sense.

"Video is unbelievably important," Gold said. "We'll be breaking every game down with Corsi numbers and zone starts, zone possession and PDO stats — tons of them. That's what you can expect in the NHL. Every second of every game is analyzed. You have to know exactly what to do in every situation, on every part of the ice."

"There's lots of room for creativity, too," Alvo said, "which is the—"

"Creativity is a buzzword," Gold said, cutting him off. "Sure there's the occasional razzle-dazzle individual effort — like once every ten games. Modern hockey is a puck possession game. Cycle down low, go hard at the net, lots of shots, rebounds, deflections. That's how goals are scored. People freak on highlight goals. I bet seventy percent of all goals are from less than three metres out."

"Might be a bit lower than that," Alvo said.

"It's closer to twenty percent," Rocket told Kyle and Nathan, who nodded.

Rocket looked over at the food table. He was still hungry, but he wasn't sure if he was allowed to get seconds.

Gold paid Alvo no attention. "Point is, you got to get in close to score — pay the price in the paint. Only problem with hockey today, if you ask me, is the idiots trying to ban fighting. I led the OHL in fighting, twice — kept things honest for my boys. This league's making it near impossible to fight, what with instigator penalties and suspensions. Think what happened to me. Some jerk drills me from behind into the boards, and I get a concussion and have to retire. That punk never would've done it if I could have dropped the gloves whenever I wanted."

"I get speared and elbowed all the time," Hoffer said. "As soon as I look at the guy he skates away. It sucks."

"Sometimes you got to drop the gloves," Cash said. "Can't let them get away with garbage, right, Jamie?"

"The Axmen don't let anyone get away with any-thing," Gold said. "We never back down — and we start the trouble. Most of the teams in the league are full of softies. Everyone wants to be a superstar; they don't like to get greasy. The Axmen are going to hit teams until it hurts, and then we'll fill the net with rubber. Right?"

"Totally," Cash said.

"We got to bang some bodies," Hoffer said.

Alvo picked away at his food.

"Don't be fooled by what you see on TV. Hockey's about passion. It's getting in a guy's face and making him afraid to touch the puck." Gold pounded the table with his fist. "No one's going to want to play us. No one. This league's going to tremble — I promise — tremble. We're going to be sipping champagne from the Memorial Cup, and we'll leave a trail of broken bones behind us. Right?"

"I'm not sure that's the best way to make the point to these boys," Alvo said drily.

Gold stood up. "Hey, guys," he said loudly. The room quieted. "I'll be watching the scrimmage today. I want to see a bit more grit and sandpaper. First scrimmage was a little polite. This is hockey. I need to see some puck hunger. Right? I need to see some anger. Right? I need to see some bodies flying around and smashing into people." He paused. "Right?" he shouted.

"Yes, sir!" the boys shouted back.

Gold winked and, with a nod at Alvo, left. Alvo didn't look up. Washington's face was stone cold.

"They should probably get ready," Alvo said.

Washington stood up. "Okay, let's quiet down. The scrimmage starts in an hour. The ice should be open soon, so you can go out when you're ready. Get in a good warm-up. You heard Mr. Gold. We want you to go full out this time."

"The lineups?" Cash asked.

"I'll speak to Mr. Gold about that. I guess they aren't quite ready yet. They'll be posted in the dressing rooms."

Kyle turned to Rocket. "Good luck, Mr. Primeau. I'm looking forward to smashing some heads and breaking some bodies at scrimmage."

"Have a good one, boys," Rocket said.

Kyle and Nathan left. Rocket finished his milk. He really could've done with another sandwich. Too late now: two people had come in to clean up.

Rocket looked over at the coaches. Washington and Alvo were still at the table. He thought about Kyle and Nathan. They had to play in this scrimmage. If he could just get Washington alone, he could ask him to switch them over to Red and give them a chance. Washington had proven to be a nice guy. Rocket tied the laces of his right shoe, then the left. Alvo kept sipping his coffee. Would he just leave?

"Is there a problem, Bryan?" Washington called out.

Rocket was the last player in the room. He stood up. "No, not at all. My shoelaces were loose."

"Okay," Washington said. "Why don't you go get your skate laces done up instead?"

"I will, Coach. Sorry. I . . ." He headed to the door.

"Does Gold have the lineups done?" Washington asked Alvo.

Alvo shrugged.

Rocket stopped at the table. Alvo or not, he had to try.

"Excuse me, Coach Washington . . . Coach Alvo. Do you have a second?" Rocket asked.

"Of course, Bryan. Have a seat," Washington said.

Rocket would've preferred to remain standing. This wasn't a big deal. He wanted to help Kyle and Nathan out, not have a long talk. He sat down.

"You did well in the race," Washington said. "Showed a lot of heart."

"Thanks. I did a lot of running this summer and . . . I felt pretty good."

"How are you enjoying camp so far?"

"Lots of fun — and a bit stressful, I guess."

"That's training camp," Washington said. "You're doing well. Play like you did in the first scrimmage, and I think you'll continue to make a strong impression."

Rocket nodded and leaned forward. "I wanted to ask if you've noticed the two guys who were leading in the race most of the time, Nathan and Kyle? They came third and fourth."

Washington didn't respond. Alvo continued to sip his coffee.

"Anyway, they're good guys and . . . I've gotten to know them and watched them in the drills and stuff, and I think we'd make a pretty sweet line."

"Which line is that?" Alvo said.

Rocket wanted to crawl under the table. Alvo downright scared him. He gathered his courage.

"Um, a line with me and Kyle Turner and Nathan Morris. Kyle's a big body, skates good, has an all-around game. Nathan's got a totally wicked shot and he can move pretty good, too. They were on Blue yesterday, but they didn't get a chance to play in the scrimmage. I watched them in the drills, and I think we could play together . . . We'd make a sweet line . . ." He left off. He was just repeating himself.

A half-smiled played across Alvo's face. "We'll think about it."

"Thanks a lot," Rocket said in a rush. He desperately wanted to go. Alvo made him unbelievably nervous.

Alvo nodded at the door. "You should get ready for the scrimmage," he said.

Rocket didn't need to be told twice. He thanked them again and hurried to his dressing room, a hollow ache in his stomach. Alvo didn't seem the type to like players interfering with the lineups, even in a scrimmage, especially fifteenth-rounders. Also, what would Gold say?

He pushed the change room door open.

"Come on in, Little Guy," Cash said. "Don't be afraid."

The hollow ache became a pain. Rocket unzipped his bag. He didn't answer Cash, but inside he was fuming.

CHAPTER 12

Rocket sidestepped his way to the middle of the bench. Kyle and Nathan moved over to make room.

"Beauty pass, bro. Backhand saucer is big time," Kyle said.

Nathan held his glove out and Rocket punched it. To his total surprise, Kyle and Nathan had been switched to Red as he'd asked. Unfortunately, it looked like the entire thing had been a waste of time. Washington had given them exactly one shift, killing a penalty, back in the first period. They'd sat the rest of the scrimmage.

"I'll talk to him again," Rocket said. "It's the third period — enough already."

Kyle shook his head. "No worries. It's enough you spoke to the coaches. It's not going to happen. We got dealt a bad hand."

"You guys killed that penalty. Blue didn't even get a shot," Rocket said.

"I think that might be our training-camp high-light," Nathan said.

"Yo, Bossy, the sniper." Washington held his hand out and Bossy gave it a swipe. "Two goals this scrimmage? You're bringing it this camp," Washington continued. "I always knew you could score. This is going to be your year. I have a feeling. Way to drive hard to the net. And nice outlet, Fryer, and good pass, Rocket."

"Thanks, Coach," Rocket said.

Washington moved off. Bossy sat down and snickered.

"What?" Rocket said.

"Suck up to the coach much?" Bossy said. He elbowed Fryer and laughed.

Rocket wanted to wipe the smile off his face. It would be like punching a mountain.

Rocket pressed his lips together. He decided to try one last time.

"Game's not over until the final whistle," he said to Kyle and Nathan. "Wait here."

"Where are we supposed to go?" Kyle said.

Rocket shuffled past Bossy and Fryer. "He wants to say thank you again," Fryer joked to Bossy.

Washington was leaning forward, his elbows on the top of the boards.

"Excuse me, Coach?" Rocket said quietly.

Washington turned his head.

"I was wondering if you'd had a chance to think about that thing we talked about in the lunchroom. Because it's getting into the third period and there's not a lot of time left . . ."

"Focus on your game," Washington said. "Leave the lines to me, please."

Rocket's face was burning. "Sure. I was just wondering . . . Sorry, Coach." He turned around and shuffled back to his spot.

"You give him your phone number?" Fryer said.

Rocket ignored him. Kyle and Nathan were looking at him intently. He could read the desperation in their eyes.

"He's going to try," he said weakly.

What else could he say? In silence, the three of them watched the play.

Cash passed to Hoffer on the left, who rang it around the boards. Gruny continued in to forecheck, while Cash and Hoffer peeled off for a change. Bourque and his left winger hopped onto the ice. Bossy and Fryer shifted to the door. Rocket gave Kyle's thigh a punch, then scrunched over to join his linemates. Cash and Hoffer sat beside Rocket. Kyle and Nathan stayed where they were. They could've been in another country. It didn't seem like they would ever get on the ice again.

"Seven minutes," Cash said. "Three more shifts each, boys. Let's get out there and get off."

Rocket tried not to roll his eyes too obviously. Cash was the king of the two-minute shift. Bourque had even made a few comments about it under his breath.

Blue got it out of their zone and came in on Red's defence. Gruny came off and Bourque's right winger went on. Rocket gave himself a shake and straightened his shoulders. Coach Sonia had been a stickler about how her players sat on the bench. "How you sit is how you play," she always said. He had to fire up. The chirping and Kyle and Nathan not playing were bringing him down. Good players couldn't let that happen.

Red gained possession. A smart pass up the middle from Rainer to Bourque got the puck out of their zone.

Bourque skated it over the red line and chipped it in deep. Then he curled toward the bench.

"That's how you change," Rocket muttered to himself. Maybe Cash would take a lesson.

"Rocket's line is up," Washington said. "Kyle, you take left. Nathan, you're on right."

"Coach? I got to get the hat trick," Bossy said.

"Save it for a real game," Washington said.

Bossy slumped back.

Rocket joyfully threw himself over the boards and stormed into Blue's end. Now they had to make something happen!

The right defenceman held the puck behind his net. Rocket stopped in the slot and waited. The guy was a right-handed shot, which meant he would probably come out the right side. Rocket shifted over a few metres. Immediately, the defenceman came out the left side and passed to his winger set up against the wall.

Bad move. Nathan crunched him against the boards and the puck squibbed back to the corner. Rocket was on it first. He turned and faced the zone. Kyle was set up at the wall by the hash marks. Rocket rang the puck around the boards to him and then scooted in behind the net. Kyle bulled his way down low to the corner, pressured by the right winger. Rocket noticed Nathan take a position in the slot. Blue's right defenceman went to the puck, but before he could get a stick on it, Kyle shoved it to Rocket.

Nathan faked right then slipped past the defenceman's left shoulder and held his stick out wide right. Rocket snapped a pass to him.

Nathan took it, and the puck became a blur. It was a bullet drive over the goalie's right shoulder. The goalie didn't move.

A goal.

Rocket jumped up in the air.

"One touch — one goal," Rocket said to Nathan. He gave his winger's pads a slap. "Shooting percentage is a pathetic one hundred percent."

Kyle and Nathan punched gloves.

"Let's not waste time celebrating," Rocket said to them. "Cash is probably crying to get on the ice."

That got their attention. They skated quickly back to centre. Rainer went over to Nathan.

"Nice snipe," he said.

Rocket liked Rainer. He never chirped at guys and he seemed fair. His defence partner, Big Z, didn't say much, but he seemed to be an okay guy, too. Rocket sneaked a glance at the Red bench. Cash was standing and talking to Washington. The coach listened impassively — no line change yet. Rocket adopted a reverse grip. He had to win the faceoff. This was Kyle and Nathan's last chance. Possession was key. His hand could feel better tomorrow. The hot beanbag had done wonders.

The referee held the puck over the dot. Blue's centre had a reverse grip also. Rocket had already gone up against him. He was fairly straight ahead on the draw. Rocket gave Nathan a glance and nodded toward the sideboards. Nathan nodded back ever so slightly. The ref blew his whistle.

Rocket changed his grip. The puck dropped. Instead of trying to draw it back, he jabbed the shaft of his stick forward to block Blue's centre, and the next second he swung his stick to whack the puck with his forehand. His right hand felt like it was on fire. Maybe he'd overestimated his healing. No time to worry about that.

Nathan retrieved the puck from the boards and swooped in on Blue's defence. Rocket hustled to support. About two metres from the blue line, Nathan lobbed the puck up high to the opposite corner. The right defenceman went back tentatively. Kyle slipped inside, lifted his stick and stole the puck. The right defenceman managed to press Kyle against the wall. Rocket went over to help and Kyle chipped the puck to him. Blue's centre came at him from the slot. Rocket waited and then gave it back to Kyle. Rocket braced himself. The centre jumped up.

Anticipating the hit, Rocket had pressed himself against the boards. The centre ended up getting the worst of it and staggered back. Rocket didn't allow himself to enjoy the sight. Kyle had fed Nathan in the other corner. Blue's left defenceman struggled with him for possession. Nathan sheltered the puck with his wide frame. Rocket circled the net and Nathan kicked it over. The cycle was on. Again and again, Rocket, Kyle and Nathan circled, pushed, fought and pressed. Again and again, they kept the Blue team at bay, first in the right corner, then the left. The few times the puck was sent to the point, Rainer and Big Z supported them by making perfect passes to either Kyle or Nathan.

Then, Rocket had the puck in the deep corner. Nathan battled in front of the net for position. Kyle drifted into the high slot. Rocket's eyes lit up. He could tell his linemates saw the opportunity, too. Rocket faked a move behind the net and cut diagonally to the faceoff circle on the goalie's right. The right defenceman covering him was too slow getting over. Rocket curled on his inside edges, dropped his left shoulder and put the puck on his backhand. The defenceman tried a poke check, but too late. The goalie came out, pads in a V, glove shoulder height. Nathan sealed off the left defenceman, clearing a path for Rocket, who brought the puck to his forehand and reared back. The left defenceman threw himself to the ice, stick extended. Rocket took one more step and whipped the puck across his body to Kyle.

The goalie dropped to a butterfly. Kyle darted right and let loose a powerful wrister. The puck clinked the post, glove-side — a goal! Kyle nodded emphatically and slapped the ice with his stick. Rocket threw his arms around Kyle's shoulders. Nathan held his arms wide and the three of them gave each other a bear hug.

"Okay, maybe this shift is the highlight," Nathan said gleefully.

"If Gold wants puck possession, then he just got it," Rocket said.

Rainer and Big Z slapped Kyle's pads.

"That was a beauty," Rainer said. "Can't cycle the puck better than that."

Big Z punched all three of their gloves, and with that the two defenceman headed to the bench.

As much as he'd love to keep playing, Rocket followed. He was tired.

"I think Cash wants a change," Rocket said to Kyle and Nathan.

Cash was already at centre.

"Two goals in one shift," Rocket said as they skated off. "I bet even Alvo is smiling now."

He could only hope that was true.

CHAPTER 13

Rocket had nowhere to go. He stood on the edge of a cliff, the ground beneath his heels crumbling. Suddenly two hands hit his chest, sending him flying backward. Rocket plunged into the abyss below, his fingers clawing at the air, his arms waving desperately. Above, he could see Connor on the edge, laughing and holding a huge boulder. Connor threw the boulder after Rocket, who kept falling faster and faster. But the boulder was faster still.

Rocket looked over his shoulder. He was about to hit the ground. When he turned back, the boulder was there. It—

"Bryan! Breakfast is ready."

Rocket sat up with a start. He was in a strange bedroom. Why?

Devin peered in. "My mom wanted me to wake you up. We're eating."

The beanbag fell off the bed onto the floor. An incredible feeling of relief washed over Rocket. No Connor. No boulder. "Devin, you saved my life. I was falling to my death in a canyon, and a huge boulder was about to crush me. One more second and I was a goner."

Devin gave him an odd look. "I've read that stress and anxiety can affect our dreams," he said. "The falling dream is common for people who are facing a lot of stress and feel like things are out of their control. Maybe there's a connection between your dream and this being the last day of training camp?"

"Um, maybe," Rocket said.

"Anyway, you should probably get going. Dad says we're leaving soon."

"No problem. I'll hustle."

Devin left. Rocket hopped out of bed and raced to the shower.

Devin was right. Rocket was totally nervous about today. Last day of training camp — D-Day. The coaches were making cuts to get down to twenty-eight players for the exhibition season.

Rocket showered quickly and towelled off. He knew worrying wouldn't help; he just didn't know how to stop. What if he didn't make the cut? Would they keep him as a reserve player in case they wanted to call him up later? Could he still get on a Junior A team for this season? And if he did make it, then what about his mom and Maddy? They'd be stuck in that neighbourhood for the next few years, and Maddy would have to watch out for Connor and the Brigade on her own. But if he *didn't* make it, he'd never get his family out of there . . .

That boulder felt real enough right now — the stress was beyond intense.

His worries still racing through his head, Rocket got dressed and went upstairs.

Strohler was at the table with Kimberly and Devin, the receiver in his ear glowing blue.

"We can't stop an NHL team from drafting Aaron," Strohler was saying. "To a certain extent it depends on the luck of the draw. If Aaron goes number one, and I think he will, then whoever wins the lottery will take him. But that's where I can help. I'll get him the best contract and set up tons of endorsements. In a year or two, you'll all be set for life."

Rocket sat next to Devin.

"Yes, Chris, you're totally right," Strohler said, rolling his eyes. "That's why we need to get him an offer sheet when he's an RFA . . ."

"What's he saying?" Kimberly said to Devin. She handed him a plate of eggs, bacon and toast.

"He's talking to Cash's dad about the NHL draft," he said.

Strohler pushed his empty glass toward Kimberly and tapped his earpiece. "I swear I'm going to kill that guy. He calls me ten times a day with questions — and then never shuts up. Brutal. Life's really fair. He knows nothing about hockey. He's as dumb as a bag of hammers, and this idiot's kid is going to make millions of dollars. Go figure. My kid can't even skate."

Devin adjusted his headphones.

Strohler shoved his glass closer to Kimberly who was pouring the boys juice. "Am I invisible? Some OJ?"

She pushed the carton to him. He grunted and poured it himself.

"What happened to Cash last night?" Strohler said to Rocket. "Why didn't he come over?"

"Yeah, sorry. He said he had something . . . something to do with his parents, I think," Rocket said.

That was a stupid thing to say. What if Strohler asked? Too late now.

"Doesn't matter," Strohler said. "I came up with a better plan, sheer genius. I invited the team over for a party tonight — the guys that make it, of course, with parents and billets. That'll get Gold on my side, and he's in tight with Cash's parents. The boys will go swimming and hit the hot tub. I might even score another client or two while I'm at it."

Kimberly put her coffee mug down. "Was I going to be told about this?"

"Relax. Had to make an executive decision. I need more time with Chris and Dawn. I'm so close, I can taste it. Seriously. This party will put me over the top."

He pointed his fork at Devin. "Get me every piece of information on Jamie Gold you can find. I mean everything. I want to know when that idiot was toilet trained. I'm serious, Devin, and do it right this time." He put his fork down. "I still can't believe Gold made the NHL. I was three times the player he was — no wait, four times — and five times tougher. We even had a fight, I think, back in Junior A. I totally whipped his butt. The guy was useless. Ridiculous I didn't get called up. Then that stupid suspension . . . I should've sued the league."

"That was so many years ago," Kimberly said.

"Not for me," Strohler said. "I'll show them who Carl Strohler is when I'm the biggest hockey agent on the planet. You wait. It starts with OHL players. Soon I'll have a bunch of NHLers on my roster. Then I'll expand to Europe and Russia. I predict Russian players are going to make a huge comeback in the NHL, and I'm going to cash in on it."

As Strohler went on about the money he would make, a new worry popped into Rocket's head. What if he got cut today? He couldn't be here for the party. It would be a total humiliation. His appetite disappeared.

"Would you like more juice?" Kimberly asked Rocket and Devin.

They held out their glasses.

"I've taken care of everything for tonight," Strohler was saying. "The caterer should be here to set up the food by five, and I told Gold to have the team come for seven. You just need to make sure the house is in order."

"I'll be at work until six today," Kimberly said.

"I think you can close your clothing store a couple hours early," Strohler said. "This is important."

"So is my store. Since you quit working for my father, I'm the only one earning money."

Strohler snorted. "I sign Cash, and the money you make from that store will be petty cash. Don't you worry about that. This is my chance. They cheated me out of millions as a player, but they can't stop me now. I'm on my way up, and no one's stopping me." He stuffed half a fried egg into his mouth.

"Can you do me a favour?" Strohler said to Kimberly, still chewing. "Buy some Diet Coke for the party. Apparently, that's all Chris drinks, and he drinks it by the bucket. He's like an addict. Get ten bottles."

Strohler reached for the orange juice. "So tell me, Bryan, you got any feel for what Cash is thinking on the agent front?"

The daily question.

"I think he's real close to making a decision," Rocket said.

Not true, but he figured that would satisfy him.

"He must've said something more specific."

"We usually talk hockey — strategy, the lines and plays . . ."

"Here's what you got to do," Strohler cut in. He didn't say it like Rocket had a choice. "Tell Cash he'd be stupid not to sign with me. Tell him that I have all the contacts, that I understand tax law, contracts and marketing and that he'll make tons of money with me. Build me up. Okay?"

"I'll try."

Strohler suddenly stood up. "We leave in seven minutes. Be ready." He tapped his earpiece. "Strohler, talk to me," he said, and he went to the hallway to take the call.

"So what's on for today?" Kimberly asked Devin.

Devin glanced into the hallway. "I think we're watching the tryout," he said.

"Maybe tonight, at the party, you can show the boys some of your games?" she said. "That might be fun."

"I doubt it," Devin said, looking down at the table. He seemed even less happy about the party than Rocket and Kimberly.

"The guys would love to play," Rocket said, hoping to cheer Devin up. "They game all the time. They'll be into it."

Devin just shrugged.

Strohler popped his head in. "I want to get there a little early," he said. "Devin, can you hurry for once in your life? You're still in your pajamas. You going to a sleepover or a hockey rink? *Come on*."

Suddenly, Devin's head was bobbing up and down to a beat Rocket couldn't hear.

Strohler threw his hands in the air. "That kid is deaf, I tell you. I'm going to throw those stupid headphones out. He never hears a word I say. Kimberly, can you get him ready?"

Devin got up and walked out.

Strohler slapped his Bluetooth receiver on. "Strohler, talk to me. Yeah. I'm looking at signing three potential first-rounders. Prepare the contracts like I told you, and we can change them if we need to . . ."

"Good luck today," Kimberly said to Rocket.

"Thanks," Rocket said, "and thanks for breakfast. That was great. I'll just brush my teeth, and I'll be ready."

Rocket went to the stairs. He heard a sound to his right and looked down the hall. Devin was standing against the wall, his arms crossed. Rocket looked over his shoulder. Strohler had gone back into the kitchen.

Rocket headed over. He could understand why a guy like Devin might not want to hang out with a bunch of guys like Cash, Hoffer and Gruny.

"Hey, Devin. Don't worry about the party," Rocket said. "It won't be a big deal. Like I said, most of the guys will game, or they'll be all over the swimming pool."

Devin just looked at him.

Rocket tried again. "Or, maybe you could hang at a friend's house tonight? Clear out until the guys are gone?"

"Friends? Yeah, maybe. Doesn't matter," Devin muttered.

Rocket wasn't making any headway, and he needed to get ready.

"Okay. Well. just an idea. See you in a sec."

He headed back down the hall.

"I have you at sixty-seven percent to make the team," Devin called out to him. "You need to have a big scrimmage today."

Rocket turned back. "Thanks. I plan to."

"Hurry up!" Strohler yelled.

Rocket raced downstairs to the bathroom.

This had to be the best hockey day of his life. Every pass perfect. Every check hard. Every shot delivered.

Sixty-seven was a high number — but it wasn't a hundred!

CHAPTER 14

Cash, Hoffer and Gruny hopped over the boards for Blue on the fly. The coaches had switched things up for this scrimmage and moved some lines around.

Rocket took a look at the scoreboard. Red 6, Blue 4. Guys were trying to get noticed and defence had taken a back seat. The poor goalies were having a tough go

On the whole, Rocket couldn't be happier. His line had been magic. Nathan had notched a goal with his killer shot, and Kyle had gotten one on a wraparound. As for himself, Rocket had scored Red's first marker in the first period on a pretty tic-tac-toe passing play in front of the net.

"I'm changing my highlight reel to this game." Kyle grinned and took a slurp of water. "You're the sweetest player I've ever played with. I'd pick you over Cash any day."

"Cash got a nice goal," Rocket said.

"You got one, too," Nathan said.

"I'll give you that," Rocket deadpanned.

His linemates laughed.

"Rockwood's line next," Washington said. "Look

alive. Let's keep the puck in their end."

Bourque's line was out, and they seemed to have heard the coach. They dumped the puck in and skated over. Rocket was over the boards first and he cruised into the Blue end. Cash's line stayed on.

A Blue defenceman skated the puck out. He dropped it to his partner, who cut right and passed to Gruny against the boards, a metre outside his blue line. Gruny banked it off the wall, with Cash flashing up the side. Kyle was there to break it up, and he and Cash scuffled for the puck. Rocket got over there and pulled the puck out from their skates. He saw a flash of red go by — Nathan.

The puck rolled on its edge. Rocket had to take a second to lay it flat, and then he snapped it to Nathan who was powering up the middle. Nathan took the pass mid-stride and bore in on goal — a breakaway.

Tweet!

Nathan slapped the ice. The referee's arm was over his head, and he was pointing to the offside dot. Rocket skated to Nathan.

"My bad. Puck was on its side. I should've got it to you faster," Rocket said.

Nathan tapped Rocket's shin pads. "Not sure I was offside. I think it was a bad call."

"Consider it a goal," Rocket said.

The referee blew his whistle. Rocket hustled to the faceoff. He'd only had two draws so far against Cash. He'd watched him all camp, though. Cash relied on his reflexes and timing — and he was good at it. He didn't like the rough stuff much, didn't like it greasy, which was precisely what Rocket had in mind.

"Hey, Little Guy, sorry this is your last scrimmage with OHL players," Cash sneered.

Rocket kept his eyes fixed on the ref's hand. The puck dropped. Cash slapped at it. Rocket blocked his stick and then knocked Cash off balance with his shoulder. It was an easy kick over to his left defenceman, who cross-iced the puck to his partner. Unfortunately, the puck hopped over the defenceman's stick. Rocket took a step that way.

"Out of my way, midget," Cash said, applying a good two-handed slash to Rocket's right hand.

Rocket bent over, holding his hand. Cash skated away.

"Sure, run away, weasel!" Rocket yelled.

His hand was in serious pain. He needed to get to the bench. But he couldn't now. They had to get the puck in deep.

He curled into the neutral zone to create space for his wingers. Red's defenceman had retrieved the errant puck and backed up with it. He looked around and swung it back to his partner. Rocket turned that way. The whistle sounded.

Rocket spun around. Cash lay on the ice. Nathan stood over him.

"Sorry," Nathan said. "You had your head down and ran into me,"

Cash got to one knee slowly. "Cheap shot, idiot. Stupid hack."

Nathan dropped his hands to his sides. "I didn't hit you. Seriously."

Hoffer came up and shoved Nathan away with a two-hander to his chest.

Nathan pushed Hoffer back. "He ran into me. Not my fault."

"Break it up, boys," the referee said.

The two linesmen pulled them apart.

"Call the penalty, ref," Cash snapped. "What were you looking at? I didn't have the puck."

The referee pointed to the bench. "Gold wants you to change," he said.

Cash slapped the ice with his stick. He gave Nathan a hard look and skated to his bench.

Hoffer skated backward. "Next shift, jerk," he said. "You're mine."

Nathan looked up at the ceiling.

"What happened?" Rocket asked him.

"I was cutting into the seam, figuring you'd get the pass, and Cash turned and skated into me. He wasn't looking," Nathan said.

"I saw it," Kyle said. "No worries — a hockey play."

It was obvious Nathan felt bad. He wasn't that type of player.

Rocket looked over to his bench, hoping for a change. Washington's arms were crossed. The one time Rocket wanted to get off and he had to stay on.

"Flush it," Rocket said. "We got to fire up again. We'll be lucky to get one more shift. We're going to make this team, all three of us. One more goal is all we need. No letting up."

Kyle slapped their shin pads and took his spot at left wing across from Fryer. Bossy ambled over next to Nathan on the right. Rocket's former linemates had been transferred to Blue, along with Cash's line, for this scrimmage.

Rocket bent down for the draw. He figured he'd try a backhand sweep to his right defence. Blue's centre put his stick down. The referee, however, was off to the side, intently studying the puck. Rocket and the other centre stood up.

"Has he never seen a puck before?" Rocket joked.

Blue's centre didn't react.

Rocket bit his lower lip. Apart from Kyle and Nathan, did anyone on this team not hate him?

"Sorry, bro, but we got to go," Bossy said to Nathan.

Rocket looked over in surprise.

"I didn't mean to hit him," Nathan said. "You saw it. He ran into me."

"Sorry," Bossy shrugged. "Orders from the top." He pushed Nathan in the chest.

"This is stupid," Nathan said.

Bossy pushed Nathan again, and then he dropped his stick and gloves and backed up, fists raised.

Nathan looked over to the referee, who still seemed fascinated with the puck. The two linesmen circled, but neither made a move to stop the fight. Nathan's face tensed and he let his stick and gloves fall to the ice, too.

The referee spun the puck in the air, caught it and backed up to the wall.

Bossy feinted a left jab, then a right hook. Nathan circled left.

"Teach the hack some manners," Cash shouted from the bench. Rocket almost laughed out loud. Who was Cash to call anyone a hack after his garbage slash?

"Kill him, Boss-Man," Hoffer added.

The players on both benches were standing.

Bossy threw a left. Nathan deflected it with his right and responded with his own jab. Bossy avoided it easily, but Nathan wasn't done. He followed immediately with another left, and then a left-right combination — the right catching Bossy on his cheek. Bossy shook his head.

Rocket was shocked when he saw Bossy's face. The guy could have been reading a book or watching television. There was no hint of anger.

Bossy pressed forward with a number of vicious jabs. Several connected. Nathan began circling right, bobbing his head and weaving. He hit Bossy with another right hand. Bossy grabbed Nathan's arm and began raining sweeping haymakers. Nathan continued to weave and he leaned as far back as he could. Suddenly, Nathan launched his own right. Bossy's head snapped back. Bossy let go of Nathan's arm and jabbed him. The punch caught Nathan by surprise. Rocket could see a trickle of blood coming from Nathan's nose.

Without warning, Bossy threw a thunderous right hook to Nathan's chin. Nathan's knees buckled, but only for a second. Then he charged Bossy and wrapped his arms around his neck. Bossy grabbed him around the shoulders. Again, Rocket noticed Bossy's face: eyes flat, no emotion.

"Let go, boys," a linesman said. He was pulling Nathan's left arm away.

Bossy released Nathan and skated directly to the penalty box. The Blue players pounded the boards with their sticks. A few Red players did the same.

Rocket went over to Nathan.

"Awesome battle," Rocket said. "Toe-to-toe with Bossy is impressive."

Nathan gave his head a shake. "What was the point of that?"

"Good work, bro," Kyle said. "We'll call it a draw."

"He got me pretty good at the end there," Nathan said, rubbing his jaw.

"Looked like a love tap to me," Kyle said.

"He must really love me." Nathan laughed. He turned toward the penalty box.

A linesman grabbed him by the arm. "You need to get checked out," he said.

Nathan shook his head. "I'm fine."

"Concussion protocol," the linesman insisted. "Coach's orders. You got stung, so you got to be checked."

Nathan tossed his hands in the air. "This is ridiculous. It was just a fight."

The linesman pushed Nathan toward the door leading to the dressing rooms.

"Get off the ice already," Cash called out.

"Shut up, jerk," Kyle yelled back.

"Any time, bud," Hoffer said, banging his stick on the boards.

"Forget them," Rocket said. "Game's almost over. Nathan did good — better than good. Gold will be impressed. Bossy's a big-time fighter. Let's change."

He and Kyle skated to the bench. Washington didn't say a word to them. Rocket sat on the bench and shifted over to make room for Kyle. The referee blew his whistle, and the centres lined up at the offside circle.

"That was a total set-up," Rocket said. "Ref did nothing, linesmen did nothing. Alvo sent Bossy to fight on purpose."

"Shhh," Kyle said. "This isn't the place."

"But I heard Bossy . . ."

"Not now, trust me," Kyle whispered.

Washington put his hands on Rocket's shoulder pads. "Settle down or you can go to the dressing room," he said, in a low, measured tone. "Understand?"

"Yes, Coach." Rocket was so angry, he was afraid to say more.

Washington moved a few steps away.

"Nathan will be fine," Kyle said. "His head is really hard. I bet Bossy hurt his hand."

Rocket wasn't ready to laugh it off.

"That was a set-up," he whispered. "No reason for it. Nathan didn't hit Cash."

He prayed Nathan didn't have a concussion. That could get him cut.

Then again, would the coaches have set Nathan up if they'd intended to keep him? Something else for Rocket to worry about as he watched the scrimmage come to an end.

128

CHAPTER 15

The cuts were about to start.

Rocket thought he might throw up right there in the dressing room, in front of everyone. It took all his willpower to hold it in.

"I could go for a clubhouse and fries at Jimmy's," Kyle said to Nathan.

They'd been talking about food for the past five minutes. It hadn't helped Rocket's stomach.

"Gravy on the fries?" Nathan said.

"You're kidding, right? The only real question is whether I get the apple pie for dessert."

Nathan's eyelids lowered. "Now I know you're kidding."

"Obviously." Kyle laughed. "I meant whether I should have two."

Rocket wished he could be chill like them. He couldn't, though. Too much riding on this. That boulder on his back had never felt bigger.

He needed a distraction. "What's Jimmy's?" he asked.

"It's a dump in town," Kyle said, "but we like it. Basically live there."

Nathan laughed.

"Jimmy's a big hockey guy — played in the AHL," Kyle said.

"There's this wicked Chinese restaurant near me, has the best barbequed duck in the world," Rocket said.

"You like living in a big city?" Kyle asked.

"It's okay," Rocket said. "My area's kind of run-down and you got to be careful of stuff. I like how you can go anywhere you want around Axton."

"What do you mean?" Nathan said.

Rocket shrugged. "Gangs and stuff. Just some people you need to avoid."

"Sounds hard-core, bro," Kyle said. "Worst thing that happens in Axton is the fries aren't hot enough."

"Cold fries are pretty bad," Nathan said.

"Cold fries are a nightmare," Kyle said. "I'd take being terrorized by gangs any day."

"Jimmy serves bad fries?" Rocket asked.

Kyle and Nathan looked shocked.

"I'm kidding, of course," Rocket said.

Kyle breathed out slowly and wiped his forehead. "Bro, I thought we were going to have to kill you."

"Maybe you should. This waiting is torture," Rocket said.

"Come on, you're in," Kyle said. "You've been dominant. You got, like, ten points in the scrimmages."

"There are really only two centre spots open, and they can only keep four sixteen-year-olds on the active roster," Rocket said. "Plus, there's a height and weight issue working against me. You heard Gold. Do I look like I wear guys down with my physical play?"

"You wear them out with your speed," Nathan said.

The door opened. All conversation stopped.

"Kyle Turner and Nathan Morris," Chen announced. "Coaches want to talk to you."

"Good timing," Kyle said. "I want to talk to them. The sandwiches at lunch today totally sucked."

All the boys laughed.

"Good luck," Rocket said.

"No worries, bro. We'll be hanging at Jimmy's later. Come by," Kyle said.

"Good luck to you, too," Nathan said.

They left.

"Three-day training camps are ridiculous," a guy across from Rocket said loudly. "How can you show your stuff in three scrimmages, especially when they switch guys around?"

"I had five different centres and three right wingers," another boy said.

"Try being in net when *everyone's* trying to score. Felt like an NHL all-star game," said Akim, one of the goalies.

Rocket couldn't imagine the pressure of being a keeper. He'd spoken to Akim a few times and knew the goalie had made the reserve team last year. Akim had even been called up for a game when Glassy got hurt. Rocket thought he was talented — real quick, good on the angles, and he had an awesome glove.

"I got to admit, I don't want to go back to my school if I'm cut," another guy said. "Everyone was like, 'You're going to the show, bro. You'll be a millionaire.' So now I'm supposed to go back and sit in geography?" He smiled weakly. "If that happens, I'm going to say I got hurt."

"Nothing wrong with playing Junior A for a year and taking another shot," Bourque said. "That's what I did. I got cut by the Battalion and made it the next year."

"Tier II is also good," someone said, "or you can play university."

"NCAA, Division I is big time."

"The NCAA won't take you if you ate lunch with us today," Bourque said. "They'll consider you a professional."

"What? We haven't even made the team," someone said.

Bourque shrugged. "Doesn't matter if you make it. After forty-eight hours at a training camp, you can't accept anything from an OHL team, and that includes billeting or food — nothing. If you make it in the OHL, though, you get a year of university tuition for each year you play. That's what I'm here for."

Rocket squeezed his hands between his knees. He hadn't exactly told his mom this. She was all stoked about his chance at getting a U.S. scholarship. But he'd always dreamed of the OHL — he figured it was his best chance to be drafted to the pros.

Chen opened the door. "Bourque, come on."

Bourque got up. "Good luck, boys. It was fun meeting you. Hopefully, we'll be on the same team or play against each other someday."

The other guys said goodbye and Bourque left.

"He's a good guy," someone said.

"No attitude, unlike another centre I know."

A few guys chuckled. Rocket kept quiet. Nice to know he wasn't the only one unimpressed with Cash's act. After this scrimmage, Rocket knew that's what it was — an act. Cash had skills; he could play. But he didn't respect the game.

Rocket leaned back against the wall. He thought about all the other times he'd sat in a dressing room waiting for someone else to decide his fate. He closed his eyes and rolled his neck forward. That boulder sure felt heavy.

Please let me make this team, he silently pleaded.

"Bryan Rockwood."

His eyes sprang open. The sound of his name blindsided him, leaving him breathless.

His future had come down to this. He thought of that smashed-up lobby door back home.

"Good luck, guys," he said.

A few boys nodded.

"Good luck," Akim called out as he left.

The walk down the hallway reminded him of a movie he'd seen with Maddy, about a man about to be executed in prison. Obviously not the same thing. It kind of felt like it, though.

"Have you enjoyed yourself?" Chen asked.

He wished she'd leave him alone. "I guess."

"It's a difficult time. The coaches hate it."

He couldn't see Gold losing sleep over it, or Alvo. Rocket looked for Kyle and Nathan. They weren't around.

"Go on in," she said. "They're waiting for you."

He pushed the door open.

"Come have a seat," Gold said.

Gold, Alvo and Washington sat behind a table. Rocket sat down across from them.

"How'd you enjoy camp?" Gold said.

"Good. Great. Lots of fun — meeting the guys and stuff." Rocket didn't know what else to say.

"Well, that's the important thing," Washington said.

Rocket wasn't sure he agreed.

Gold slid his iPad away. "We're trying to create an NHL-level experience for you guys, something for you to remember and take with you for the rest of your lives."

Rocket nodded silently.

Gold sat back in his chair. "You did well at fitness. You also skate well and see the ice. Good puck distribution. Good skill set. Need work on the physical side. Your Corsi numbers were good, though, very good. Do you understand what that means?"

"Yes, sir."

Probably not the time to tell them he was a sports trivia expert. He knew Corsi measured puck possession by comparing how many shots your team had when you were on the ice versus how many it gave up, including missed and blocked shots.

"How do you think you did?" Washington said.

Rocket interlocked his fingers and pushed the tops of his hands into his thighs. How to answer that question without sounding too full of himself?

"I think I can play in this league and help Axton. I know I'm not the biggest guy. But I've been dealing with that my whole life, and I know how to compete against bigger bodies. I'll do whatever it takes to win. I just want to learn and get better and . . . My dad's tall, so I think in a few years . . ."

He squeezed his fingers. Stupid thing to say. Like they'd believe him.

Alvo was stone-faced, as always. Rocket looked at Washington. He seemed concerned.

Gold leaned forward. "You're an interesting project, Rockwood. I got to be honest. Stats are important, for sure. I'm totally committed to modern hockey. At the same time, hockey is a physical game. We're building something special here. We're focused on championships, Memorial Cups — winning. We need special players to do that, guys with size who can pound the other team." He sat up straight. "I didn't necessarily see you fitting the Axton model. Like you just said, you're not the biggest kid in the world. You're a skill guy — and we have a few of those already."

It was all Rocket could do to sit still.

"Fortunately, for you, I've been outvoted," Gold said. "Go figure. I buy the team and I can't even choose the players."

Gold laughed like crazy. Washington joined in. Alvo remained quiet.

"We went hard at it — fists almost flew, I can tell you — but in the end, you won out," Gold said.

Rocket stared at him.

"You made the cut, kid," Gold said. "Congrats for now. We'll see what you can do in the exhibition season."

Rocket gasped and the men laughed. He'd been holding his breath. "Thanks. Sorry. I was . . . a bit nervous," he said.

"We thought you played well with Bossy and Fryer," Gold said. "We'll probably go with that and see how you do. They're big bodies, and they'll make sure nobody takes any liberties."

"Yes, sir. Thank you, sir."

They were interrupted by a knock on the door. Chen popped her head in.

"Are we ready?" she said.

"Send him in," Gold said.

Alvo held out his hand. Rocket reached out tentatively and shook it. Alvo had a solid grip.

"We have a team dinner tonight at seven," Gold said. "Here are the details." He handed over a piece of paper.

"I'm staying with the Strohlers, so . . ."

"That's right. Forgot. Couldn't have worked out better for you," Gold said. He poked his iPad a few times and showed Alvo the screen.

"Thanks again," Rocket said, his voice quivering slightly. "I won't let you down."

"Keep putting in that effort," Washington said.

Rocket smiled back at him, trying to convey his immense gratitude. Washington had stood up to Gold — again. Rocket pushed the door open, and another player walked in as he went out.

He was alone in the hallway, so he stopped to take another deep breath. That boulder on his back felt a lot lighter — at least for now. He had the exhibition season to prove himself. Six games to take the first big step toward the NHL.

He pulled out his phone and texted a message to his mom and Maddy — they had a lot riding on this, too. Then he added Megan, André, Ty and the guys on the trivia team.

Survived training camp. Exhibition season here I come.

Maddy answered right away.

So what? You're still a loser. I'm coming to see your game in Axton. Set it up.

Rocket texted his answer as he walked to the lobby. His head felt like it was floating; his feet seemed to barely to touch the floor.

Awesome, sis. Looking forward to being cooler than you.

CHAPTER 16

The man came into the house carrying a fruit tray. He'd been bringing in food for fifteen minutes. Kimberly followed him in.

"You could've told me you were here," she said to Strohler. "I didn't need to close up. I actually had to tell some customers to leave." She looked around. "How much food did you order?"

"Can't look cheap. Chris and Dawn will be judging every move I make," Strohler said.

"Who are they again?" she asked.

"Cash's parents," Strohler said. "Please engage. Now, did you buy the Diet Coke?"

"Yes. Three bottles."

"Three! I told you to get ten."

"No human being can drink ten 2-litre bottles of Coke."

"If we run out, I swear . . ." Strohler touched his earpiece. "Jamie! What's up?" He walked into the kitchen.

"Is there anything we can do to help?" Rocket asked Kimberly.

"You're sweet. I think we're okay. It seems we have

enough food to feed ten hockey teams," Kimberly said.

"What time are they coming, again?" Devin said.

"They're not," Strohler snapped, stomping back into the hallway.

"What do you mean?" Kimberly asked.

"Stupid Gold cancelled," he fumed. "Apparently, his friends are in town. He wants to do it next week."

"But we have all this food!" Kimberly said.

"No kidding."

"Tell this Mr. Gold to bring his friends here," Kimberly said.

"Geez, Kimberly. You want me to look pathetic and beg? They want to do it next week."

"But we have all the food *now*."

The caterer walked in carrying two cakes.

"This isn't what we ordered," Strohler roared.

The man froze. "I emailed the order to you and you confirmed it."

"Take it all back. These sandwiches aren't fresh. The bread is gross and soggy and the cheese smells." Strohler sniffed the air and gagged.

"I can assure you the food was prepared fresh today. We have a reputation . . ."

"Get this cat food out of here," Strohler said. "I'm not paying for any of this garbage, either. I have events catered all the time. You can't fool me."

"Maybe you should go hang out downstairs," Kimberly whispered to Rocket and Devin. "Dinner won't be for a while. I'll call you when it's ready."

Rocket thought that was a very good idea. Apparently, Devin did, too. They crept over to the stairs.

Then Rocket remembered that Maddy wanted to

come up for a game. He crept back to look for Kimberly, who had escaped to the living room.

"Kimberley," he whispered, "would it be okay if my sister came up and stayed a night? She wants to see me play a game before school starts." He figured it would be easiest to pretend they were actually related.

"Of course," she said. "Just let me know when."

"I wouldn't feed this to my dog!" Strohler was shouting.

"Someone needs to pay for it," the man said angrily.

Rocket hurried downstairs. Devin was waiting for him.

"Is he really not going to pay?" Rocket asked.

"My dad's the king of the scammers. He'll pull it off," Devin said.

"So, do you want to game?" Rocket asked.

Devin shrugged.

"We don't have to," Rocket said. "I'm up for whatever."

"Congratulations on making the team," Devin said.

"I haven't exactly made it, yet. I get to play the exhibition games," Rocket said.

"Right." Devin looked out the window.

"You feel like swimming?" Rocket said.

"If you want."

"Hey, have heard of a place called Jimmy's?" Rocket said. "We could have a pre-dinner snack. I heard the fries are legendary."

Devin put a hand to his chin. "They are good, I'll give you that. I'd be up for a walk. It's not far — ten minutes."

"Let's do it."

"Okay. I'll just tell my mom where we're going."

A few minutes later, they were on the main street.

"I told my mom we'd be late," Devin said.

"We don't have to stay long," Rocket said.

"Trust me. We don't want to be home. Dad will be on the warpath." Devin looked at the ground. "He wasn't always like this. He's just gotten obsessed over being a hockey agent. I think he feels cheated out of a hockey career and . . ." His voice trailed off.

Devin's family lived in the most beautiful house Rocket had ever seen. They had two cars, four televisions, a swimming pool, a sauna, a steam room, pool and Ping-Pong tables — basically anything a guy could want. Despite all of that, Rocket felt sorry for him. It seemed like Devin didn't have the one thing he wanted — a dad who cared about him.

Maybe that's why Rocket and Devin got along. They sort of had that in common. Rocket had seen less and less of his own dad over the years. He hadn't even called to wish Rocket luck on the tryouts.

"How come your dad feels cheated?" Rocket asked Devin.

"He was playing in the AHL and he got into a big brawl. I think he jumped off the bench and went after some guy with his stick. He hurt him bad. Anyway, he got suspended for the rest of that season and half of the next, and that's when I was born. My grandfather offered him a job, my mom's dad, that is, and he took it. After a year or two, he was making good money and had to support a family, so he gave up hockey. I think he feels his hockey career was taken from him by . . . Well, I guess he thinks he's owed something."

"Looks like he did okay."

"That's not how he feels." Devin pointed across the street. "There's Jimmy's."

Rocket could see the sign hanging from the building. They went in.

The walls were covered in posters, pennants and newspaper articles featuring athletes from all sports, but mostly hockey. There were several televisions, too. Rocket spotted a sign: *The Path to Jimmy's Most Awesome Patio.*

"You want to sit outside?" he asked Devin, who nodded.

Rocket poked his head out and saw his friends.

"Rocket! Bro! You found it."

Kyle and Nathan waved to him from a corner table.

"No one can resist the power of Jimmy's fries," Kyle said. "Have a seat. We'll score you a basket."

Rocket was at a loss for words. Did they make it? Were they here because the party had been cancelled — or did they not even know about it? He sat down, then noticed Devin standing off to the side.

"Sorry, this is Devin. He's the son of . . . he's lives at . . . I'm staying at his place," Rocket said.

"We'll said, young man," Kyle laughed.

"Yo, Devin. What's up?" Nathan said. "Have a seat."

Devin sat at the table.

Kyle waved at a waiter. "Hey, Caroline. We need two more fries, one poutine, one regular — and some more ketchup. This one's empty."

"One order of fries is enough," Rocket said. He didn't have much money.

"No worries. I got ya. Like I said, we practically run the place," Kyle said.

Caroline came over. "Do you guys need anything else? More drinks?"

Kyle held up his empty glass. "When did you become a mind reader? A round of drinks, please. What do you want, Devin?"

"Maybe a Coke?"

Kyle pointed at Rocket.

"Sure, the same," Rocket said.

"Four Cokes, Caroline. Thanks."

"Got it," Caroline said. "Give me a sec."

"Take your time. We aren't going anywhere," Kyle said.

"That's the truth," Nathan said glumly.

Rocket forced himself not to react. That was that: they'd been cut.

Caroline patted Nathan on the back. "You need food. Trust me, I'm a mind reader. You all need something good to eat. Leave it with me." She disappeared back into the restaurant.

"You're breaking your promise, bro," Kyle said to Nathan.

Nathan looked at Rocket. "They decided one free agent walk-on was enough. Kyle made the cut. I didn't. I promised myself not to let it get me down — maybe it's a promise I can't keep."

"It's not over, bro," Kyle said. "This is just another bump in the road, like a defenceman in the way of the puck. Fight through it and get the puck. Tell him, Rocket."

Nathan slowly traced the top of his glass with the tip

of his finger. "Not sure this is a bump. I think it's a dead end. Time for me to face it. I'm not going to play in the OHL, and I'm not getting drafted to the NHL."

"You can't say that . . ." Kyle began.

"I can. Maybe I play Junior A again and make it as an overage junior. Then what? The East Coast League? Or, if I'm lucky, the AHL? Then I turn twenty-five, and I have no education and I'm probably banged up. I don't have the wheels, Kyle. Never will. I can shoot. Okay. But I don't have Rocket's skills, and I don't have your skating, checking and size. Maybe I don't care enough. It's okay. It is. I'm bummed out a bit, of course." He grinned and sat back in his chair. "But it's not like my life is over."

"According to an article I read, the odds of a ten-year-old making the NHL in this province are about 3,000 to 1. The odds of playing over four hundred games and qualifying for an NHL pension are about 5,000 to 1. The odds of an OHL player going on to play even one NHL game are about 20 to 1," Devin said.

The street hummed with passing cars. The midday sun was gone, but the air was still hot and stuffy.

Kyle looked over at Devin. "Are you sure about those stats?"

"They're based on a specific birth year, but it may be even harder to break in to the NHL these days," Devin said.

"Devin's usually not wrong about stuff like this," Rocket said.

Kyle nodded meaningfully. "Something tells me you're right. So what the heck have I been doing with my life? 3000 to 1?"

Rocket turned to Nathan. "I think you should've made it. They didn't give you a chance, and that fight was unfair."

"I'm not going to miss that part of the game," Nathan said, rubbing his jaw gingerly.

Kyle gave Rocket's arm a light punch. "You're in, right?"

"By the hair of my chinny-chin-chin," Rocket said. He didn't want to talk about it in front of Nathan. "They want big bodies — story of my life. Washington stuck up for me, and they're giving me the exhibition season — with Bossy and Fryer."

"Bossy's okay," Nathan said. "He has a job to do. I think he could've killed me if he wanted."

Rocket thought back to the look on Bossy's face during the fight. "I don't think he likes being the designated goon. He does it because it's expected, but I think he hates it."

"Comes down to what price you want to pay, I guess," Nathan said.

Caroline put two baskets of fries on the table. Behind her a large, round-faced man held two platters of wings. He put them next to the fries.

"Jimmy, say hi to the one-and-only Rocket Rockwood," Kyle said, "and his friend, Devin."

"Nice to meet you," Jimmy said, in a booming, friendly voice. "The boys tell me you can really wheel out there," he said to Rocket.

"We had fun playing together," Rocket said. "These guys are awesome. They both got goals in the last two scrimmages we had."

Jimmy cuffed Nathan on the shoulder. "My boy can

shoot the lights out. He also tells me you helped him out — I appreciate that. You're welcome here anytime." He turned and held out his big fist to Kyle, who gave it a punch. "You go hard tomorrow, every shift. Bang some bodies and make yourself seen."

"Okay, Dad," Nathan said, rolling his eyes. "Let the guy enjoy the night."

Dad? Jimmy was Nathan's father.

Jimmy's laugh exploded from him. "I'm real proud of Kyle — and you, too, Nate," he said. "You gave it an honest effort. That's all I expect. You did good."

Nathan coloured. Obviously his dad's praise meant a lot to him. It was hard not to compare them to Strohler and Devin.

"Enjoy the food and let me know if you need more," Jimmy said.

He and Caroline went back into the restaurant.

"You didn't tell me the famous Jimmy was your dad," Rocket said.

"He opened the restaurant after he stopped playing," Nathan said. "I'm going to study business in school, and maybe we can open another one — at least that's my plan."

"Please open a chain of them," Kyle said. "Then I can eat free everywhere I go."

"Forget that," Nathan said. "No freebies."

"Jerk."

Nathan pushed a platter of wings to Devin. "These are hot — the others are suicide. The hot will blow your head off, so beware."

Devin reached for a suicide.

"I like this guy," Kyle said. "Knows how to live."

He took a suicide wing, too.

Caroline came over with the drinks.

Rocket didn't want to look like a wuss. He picked up a hot wing and took a bite — and reached desperately for his drink. "That's insane," he gasped, his eyes watering.

The others were laughing.

"Did you make him have a suicide?" Caroline asked.

Rocket choked and then sneezed violently a few times. Caroline patted him on the back.

"It was only a hot," Kyle said. "He's the sensitive type."

"Don't listen to these guys. Even the hot wings are deadly unless you're used to them. Are you okay?" Caroline asked.

Rocket took a few deep breaths. "I think so," he rasped.

"I'll bring you a plate of mild — or would you like honey-garlic?" she asked.

"Mild is fine, thanks."

"Could you bring some wuss-sauce as well?" Kyle said.

That sent Nathan and Devin into hysterics. Rocket joined in. He really was pathetic when it came to spicy food.

"Shush you." Caroline slapped the top of Kyle's head, and he laughed even harder.

Devin took another wing. "So what happens now that training camp is over?"

"We have a game tomorrow afternoon, against London," Kyle said.

Rocket gasped. "Are you serious? I didn't know we're playing them. The London Knights? Are you sure?"

"Um . . . yeah," Kyle said.

"My friend Ty plays for them," Rocket said. "I grew up playing with him. Awesome player. Right wing or centre. Think of Cash, but not an idiot. He went in the first round, too."

"It's crazy you have a game already," Devin said.

"True that," Kyle said. "It's a brutal bus ride, too, like seven hours. Game's at two o'clock. We won't be home until after midnight. Then they come here for a game."

Caroline put a small plate of wings next to Rocket. "Here you go, dear. These will be better."

She patted Rocket on the back.

"Has anyone ever ordered mild wings before, Caroline?" Kyle asked.

"Oh, you're such a funny guy, aren't you?" Caroline chided.

Rocket took a bite of his wings. "They're good. Thanks."

She nodded and left.

Nathan raised his Coke in the air. *"Go Axmen Go!"* he chanted.

They clinked glasses.

Rocket took another bite. This was fun, but he knew it was too early to celebrate.

Things would get serious, real serious, when the puck dropped against the Knights.

Nathan may have been cut, but at least he had his dad's restaurant.

Rocket didn't have anything. This was his shot. All or nothing.

And he wanted it all.

CHAPTER 17

Rocket ran his finger down the page until he spotted his friend's name: *Tyler Hopkins, No. 9: 5'10", 172 lbs; right wing/centre; shoots right; fast; good playmaker; physical player*. It was hard to believe he was reading about Ty in a scouting report.

"In your binders, you'll also see some basic breakouts and forechecking schemes we want to focus on in this game," Gold said. "We're going to start a new tradition this season. On road trips, before a game, you're going to sit with your lines or your defence partners and review the game sheets, especially the scouting report. Guys who aren't playing today can come up to the front."

"Perfect," Kyle laughed. "I don't have to move."

The veterans had taken over the seats in the back of the bus. The rookies took the front. No one had told them to: it was understood. Rocket didn't mind. A guy had to pay his dues.

Except for Cash. He was hanging back there with Hoffer and Gruny.

"You'll play at home against the Knights," Rocket said to Kyle.

"If they suck enough, for sure," Kyle said.

"I didn't mean that . . . It's probably a numbers thing. We have extra guys and . . ."

"I'm messing with ya." Kyle grinned. "Take a hike, and say hi to my buds Bossy and Fryer — and Cash."

"If I don't make it back alive, you can have my sticks," Rocket said.

"Too small for me, bro."

"You really are messing with me."

"Got to keep you humble."

"Hurry up, boys," Gold said. "This isn't so hard. Find your linemates, sit with them and review the package. You've had these binders since the start of training camp. I bet most of you haven't so much as cracked them open. There'll be a test soon and you better have them memorized. I'm serious."

Rocket had spent hours poring over his binder, so he wasn't worried. He *was* worried about going to the back of the bus. He looked over the top of the seats. Bossy and Fryer were in the second-last row. He swallowed hard.

Cash noticed him first. He was in the back row with Hoffer and Gruny. He clapped his hands. "I got it, Bossy. The perfect name for your line — Two-and-a-Half Men."

The guys roared.

"C'mon, Little Guy," Fryer said. He reached across the aisle and patted the seat. "We got to talk strategy. Gold's orders."

Rocket gritted his teeth and sat down.

Hoffer waved his binder in the air. "Remember that number 14 from last season? Didn't you have a tussle with him, Boss-Man?" he said.

"He was like, 'Coach is making me fight. Don't kill me, please,'" Bossy said in a high-pitched voice.

"Was he the guy who called you sir?" Gruny said.

"He called for his mommy, I remember that," Bossy said.

"Is this hockey talk?" Gold stood in the aisle.

"They were telling me about the players to watch for — guys from last season," Cash said.

Hoffer giggled and slunk behind a chair.

Gold looked around, uncertain. "Good idea. Experience is key. You younger guys need to listen up." He eyed Rocket.

Rocket prayed he wouldn't say something to him.

"Washington told me you used to play with that Tyler Hopkins kid," Gold said. "He's from your hometown, no?"

Rocket nodded.

"He's a hotshot — huge rep," Gold said. "We talked about drafting him."

"Cash, I thought you were a hotshot," Hoffer said.

"I'll smoke him," Cash said. "I played him in a tournament. He's totally soft. Needs a map to find the corners."

Rocket couldn't keep it in. "Ty's an awesome player. He doesn't back down from anyone. You got to keep your head up when he's on the ice."

Rocket could feel Cash's icy stare boring into him.

"Let's not be so impressed with the opposing players, Rockwood. We've got enough talent in this bus to beat anyone. We'll see how tough this Tyler Hopkins is after we rattle him against the boards a few times." Gold slapped his binder with his hand. "We arrive in less than an hour. Get focused." He whirled and went back to the front.

Rocket stared at the back of the seat and waited for it.

"You telling me how to play, Little Guy?" Cash said.

"I think he is," Hoffer said. "I heard him say he should be the number one centre."

Rocket didn't take the bait.

Cash came over to his seat. "What do you think, boys? Would Little Guy look better without any hair?" He patted Rocket's head. Rocket slapped his hand away.

"Little Guy is sensitive," Cash sneered. "No touchies."

"I was thinking of a tape job, but you might have something there," Hoffer said.

"The shave it is," Gruny declared, a gleeful tone in his voice.

Cash patted Rocket's arm. "We'll see you after the game," he said. "Consider it a date."

Bossy and Fryer were talking to each other, paying no attention. Cash sat back down.

Rocket's eyes blurred, his head flooded with fear — and anger. He couldn't fight them all off, but he also couldn't back down. The bullying would never stop if they thought he was scared. He gripped the armrests and turned to face the back.

"My prediction is that Ty smokes you," Rocket said in a loud voice. "You have no clue, and you're not half as good as you think you are. You think *he's* soft? I dare — no, make that double-dare — you to drop your gloves with Ty. I'd pay to see it. You'll flop on the ice like you did with Nathan. So bite me."

He tucked his binder under his arm. "We finished

talking strategy?" he said to Bossy and Fryer.

Bossy glanced over, his lips in a slight smile. Fryer didn't take his eyes off his binder.

Rocket went back to his seat. His chest was tight and he found it hard to breath. Akim was standing in the aisle talking to Kyle.

"You guys are good," Kyle said to Rocket. "You memorized everything in three minutes? You must be ready for the advanced plays."

"I guess."

The smile left Kyle's face. "You know Akim?" he said.

"Of course," Rocket said.

"You must be stoked for the game," Akim said.

"Absolutely — if we ever get there." The game wasn't exactly on his mind right now.

Kyle flipped to a page in his binder. "What's your opinion of the D-to-D Drop Pass Breakout?"

Rocket turned to that play. One defenceman took it out from behind the net, while his partner trailed behind him. At the same time, the centre curled in the slot and the wingers broke for open ice.

"I like this play," Akim said. "The puck carrier has choices: keep skating, drop it to his defence partner, pass to the left winger or centre or swing it cross ice."

"The centre's got to anticipate the drop pass and veer off the right way," Kyle said.

"The first defenceman doesn't have to drop pass," Rocket said. "Tons of variations off this."

"Check this one out," Kyle said, pointing to the diagram at the bottom of his page — The Breakaway. "I need to get me some of that action."

Rocket turned to it. It was a play off a draw in their

own end. The centre drew it back to a defenceman. The centre then peeled off and set up beside the net. The defenceman gave it back to the centre. The centre then looked to his winger, who was cutting off the wall into the middle of the ice, and sent him a breakaway pass.

Rocket figured he may as well focus on the game. For an instant he thought about telling Kyle about what had happened. He looked back. Better not. If the coaches got word of it, everyone would think Rocket had squealed, and he'd become the team punching bag. He could tough it out. They were bluffing, anyway. The league had made a big deal about stopping hazing, and there was even a section in their binders about it. Cash and his friends would get in huge trouble.

"You can run that with either winger," Rocket said, "depending where their defence is positioned."

Rocket pointed to the left winger in the diagram. His finger shook slightly as he showed them what he meant.

CHAPTER 18

"Ladies and gentlemen, put your hands together for your London Knights!"

The arena erupted in cheers, the fans on their feet, as the Knights tore onto the ice. Spotlights danced around the giant emblem at centre.

Rocket pushed off on his inside edge to carve a wide circle behind the net. His nerves were jumping at an all-time high. The arena was almost full — nine thousand people.

He circled at the top of the neutral zone and sliced the dot in half with his blade. Last out of the room, elbow pads before shoulder pads — he couldn't do anything more to get the hockey gods on his side.

"Rocket, how wild is this?"

Ty was against the boards, stick held across his waist, wearing a grin that seemed too big for his face.

Rocket skidded to a stop on one skate and slapped Ty's shin pads.

"A little different from Mooreville Park Arena," Rocket said. They'd played there when they were younger.

"Just a little. How was camp?" Ty said.

"Totally intense. I think I'm still on the bubble 'cause of my size."

"You'll make it. They only have to see you play."

They'd always been each other's biggest fans.

"How was your camp?" Rocket said.

Ty laughed. "What can I say? It was hockey, hockey, hockey. Fun, though. Good group of guys. Ad-man's doing good, too. I think he plays his first game tomorrow."

"He texted me."

Ty slapped Rocket's shin pads. "Have a good one, bud."

"Bring it," Rocket said, before skating off along the wall.

Hard not to be jealous. It sounded like Ty had a great time at camp — no way he had to worry about getting his head shaved.

The music blared. Rocket let it fire him up and he took off behind the net. He was done worrying. He had a game to play.

"Rockwood!" Gold yelled.

Rocket stopped and went to the bench. "Yes, sir?"

Gold's eyes narrowed and the veins in his neck bulged. "What colour is your jersey?"

Rocket felt sick.

"What colour is your jersey?" Gold repeated.

"Black, red and white."

"Are you wearing London Knights colours?"

"No, sir."

"Have I made my point?"

"Yes, sir."

Alvo came over. "Continue warming up, please," he said.

Gold stepped away. Rocket skated hard around the ice. Gold didn't understand. He'd try harder than anyone to beat Ty. They were like that, always pushing each other to be the best.

Somehow Rocket always managed to say or do the wrong thing around Gold. Alvo obviously saw what happened, too.

The siren sounded and the fans started to roar. The game was about to begin. The players on both sides filed into their respective benches.

Rocket was on the fourth line and would be out last. Cash's line had drawn the starting assignment — against Ty.

The national anthem played, the players swaying back and forth, shifting from foot to foot, waiting for the song to end. After what felt like forever, the whistle blew and the game began. The first few minutes were ragged, each team feeling the other out. Rocket began to prepare himself as the third line hopped the boards.

"Cash, get ready. Your line is next," Washington barked.

Bossy kicked the boards with his skate. Fryer slid back down the bench. Rocket followed in a daze. Did they not trust him because he spoke to Ty?

"Tight game, boys," Washington said. "We need to keep our feet moving — and more energy, please."

Rocket felt his energy disappear. He watched shift after shift. The teams continued to show their jitters, with missed passes and wide shots.

"Just like last year," Bossy said to Fryer. "Sit on our

butts all game until they want a fight. Coach said it would be different."

He sounded more like a disappointed kid than a dangerous fighter. Rocket sneaked a look. Bossy's face was blank and his eyes were dull.

Eight minutes were left in the first period. The Knights were up by one, a power-play marker.

A referee stopped by their bench. He reached over and helped himself to a squirt of water.

"I thought I saw a hold, ref," Alvo said.

The ref laughed. "Hey, Coach. How's it going? Looks like a good squad this year."

"Not if we play like this," Alvo said.

"First exhibition game." The referee shrugged and skated off.

Rocket hadn't seen that side of Alvo before. He'd sounded almost human.

The third line went out to replace Bourque's.

"Rockwood's line next," Washington said.

Rocket felt a surge of adrenalin race through him. His line moved to the door.

"Don't be afraid to mix it up out there," Gold said to Bossy and Fryer. "We need our energy line to make something happen."

Bossy grunted and lowered his head.

"You get me, Bossy?"

"Yeah," Bossy said without looking up.

Gold slapped his shoulder pads. "Let's start working, Axmen. Hit someone. Take the body. We're playing like little boys. C'mon!"

Rocket hated having Gold behind the bench. All he did was scream at them to "take the body" — and he was constantly abusing the refs. He reminded Rocket of those out-of-control fathers in minor hockey.

Again, Rocket sneaked a glance at Bossy. His face was still expressionless. Impossible to know what he was really thinking. Rocket had a hunch he wanted Gold and Alvo to give him a chance to prove he was more than a brawler — to let him play the game.

Rocket thought about what Gold had said — the energy line should make something happen.

"What do you guys think of The Breakaway?" he said to Bossy and Fryer. The puck was in the Axmen's end. If there was a whistle, their line could run it.

"I like it when I have one," Bossy said.

"No — the breakout play called The Breakaway," Rocket said.

"Seriously?" Fryer said.

"They won't expect it. They'll probably think you two are out to start a fight. So, whoever's against the boards on a draw in our end, let's say it's Bossy, you mess around with their winger, as if you want to drop the gloves. If I win the draw, I'll pass it to Rainer on D. Bossy, you head up the wall, and then when Rainer passes the puck back to me, you cut into the gap between the Knights' defencemen, about two or three metres over the blue line. I'll hit you with the pass. It's going up the middle, so it'll be hard. I'll have to saucer it."

On the ice, Glassy caught a weak shot from the point and held on for a faceoff.

"Okay?" Rocket said. "Do you get it?"

"Not that complicated, Little Guy," Bossy said.

Rocket stood up. "Then do it," he snapped.

Fourth-line guys shouldn't be so arrogant, even if they were veterans.

"Change 'em," Washington said.

Rocket hopped out the door and took a few quick strides to loosen his legs. He had no idea if his linemates would do the play. In any event, Bossy was the one against the boards. He'd get the breakaway, if it worked out.

Rocket had to win that draw, though. He flexed the fingers of his right hand.

"Get ready for more pain," he said under his breath.

He ducked over to Rainer. "Set up more in the corner. I'm going to pull the draw to you. Look for me on Glassy's glove side. We're running The Breakaway."

Rainer raised an eyebrow, then nodded.

The referee blew the whistle.

Bossy shoved the Knights' right winger. He shoved back. Was Bossy going to do the play — or he was setting up a fight? Rocket glided to the circle and put his blade down. The referee held the puck out. Bossy and the winger crossed sticks and pushed against each other. The Knights' centre moved his stick. The referee stood up and pointed out of the circle.

"I barely flinched," the centre said.

"Move it," the referee said.

The left winger took his spot.

This was perfect. Rocket forced himself to relax, so he wouldn't give the play away. He had a way better chance of winning the draw against a winger. The referee held the puck out. Rocket's eyes remained fixed on the ref's hand. The next instant, the puck dropped. Rocket drove his right hand forward and his left hand back and, using his momentum, spun toward the net.

Step one: win the draw. Check.

Rainer had the puck. The Knights' centre extended his stick toward it. Rainer held onto it and then slipped it deftly to Rocket by the post.

Step two: get puck back from defenceman. Check.

Bossy broke off in between the Knights' defence. Rocket fired the puck up.

Step three: pass for the breakaway. Check.

Bossy took the puck in full stride and powered down the ice. The defence had been caught flat-footed and they were five metres behind. Bossy crossed the blue line, the crowd roaring and begging their goalie to stop it. Bossy faked a shot at the hash marks, took two more strides, faked a forehand, brought it over to his backhand and then slipped the puck between the goalie's pads, five-hole.

Step four: score. Check!

The crowd groaned. A few Axmen supporters jumped to their feet to celebrate.

On their bench, the Axmen banged the boards with their sticks and high-fived each other. Rocket's linemates headed over to slap gloves. Rocket followed self-consciously, head down. He slapped everyone's gloves and went to centre for the draw.

The linesman gave the referee the puck. The Knights' centre set up. Rocket got himself ready. The puck fell and their sticks clashed — and again Rocket won the draw. Unfortunately, the puck went between the defence and into the Axmen's zone. Rainer swung wide with the puck, skating backward, and then drilled it cross ice to Big Z. Rocket curled in the neutral zone and accepted the outlet pass. The Knights' left winger lunged at him. Rocket had too much speed, and he easily avoided the winger's stick.

Rocket crossed the red line and lofted the puck toward Bossy in the corner, figuring the defenceman wouldn't want to take a hit from Bossy. Rocket was right. The defenceman tried to drag the puck with the tip of his stick. Bossy banged him off it.

Fryer flew in from the right side. Bossy continued up the wall to the hash marks. On a hunch, Rocket went to the opposite corner. Bossy rang it around. Rocket couldn't resist a smile as he gathered the puck in. That Bossy could play. The Knights' centre and left winger pressed down. Rocket banked the puck off the wall to Big Z at the point. Both Knights turned to charge Big Z, who sent it right back to Rocket in the corner.

Rocket exploded toward the front of the net, hoping to catch the Knights by surprise. The goalie reacted by dropping into his butterfly and pressing his body against the post. Fryer battled for position in the high slot with the right winger. The right defenceman had Bossy by the far post. The left defenceman lowered his hands and laid his stick across the ice to block any pass. Rocket considered cutting back behind the net and setting up the cycle with Bossy. Then Bossy backed away from the post, and the right defenceman, thinking Rocket had no play in front, drifted closer to the middle of the net.

Rocket lowered his right hand and tipped the puck on his blade. It was a crazy idea, but he did it almost instinctively. He hopped over the left defenceman's stick with the puck balanced on his blade — and the crowd went insane. The goalie pushed off the post and extended his legs to cover the bottom of the net. The right defenceman took a step forward and lowered his shoulder. He ploughed into Rocket's chest. Rocket's knees buckled and he fell, but not before he'd flicked the puck over to Bossy. Rocket hit the ice and rolled. The groan of the crowd took the hurt away. Bossy had put the puck in the net.

He felt a hand under his arm pulling him to his feet.

"Two goals in one shift," Fryer said to him. "Maybe Alvo will put us on the ice once in a while."

Bossy gave them both a big bear hug. "Awesome forecheck, boys," he said.

Rainer and Big Z joined in. Rocket felt ridiculous trapped in the middle of this group hug, but there was no escape.

"Good puck movement," Rainer said.

"Net presence, boys. Net presence," Fryer said.

Finally, the guys peeled off. Cash's line was already at centre. Rocket went to the bench.

Bossy got a hero's welcome, the guys pounding him on the back and helmet.

"Mr. Superstar."

"The beard is working its magic."

"Way to snipe a pair, bro."

Rocket took his place quietly. Two goals took the sting out of his throbbing hand.

Bossy sat down with a loud sigh. "I haven't had two goals in one shift since . . ." He paused and then laughed, "since never." He punched Rocket's knee. "Good passes," he said.

Washington crouched behind him. "Well done,

Bossy. We hoped this would continue after camp. Great finishing — and great passing, Rocket."

Rocket reached for some water. Nice for the coach to say that — and for the other boys to hear. Hopefully Fryer was right and Alvo would let them back on the ice sooner than later.

The play went end-to-end for the next minute, the two teams trading scoring chances. Ty had the puck in the Axmen's end. Cash extended his stick at the puck. Ty slipped it between Cash's stick and feet and then danced sideways and went by him. The left defenceman dropped to his knees to block the shot. Ty dragged the puck with his forehand to bring the puck to the outside of the defenceman's left shoulder and fired a wicked snapper over Glassy's glove hand.

Just like that, they were tied again.

"Change 'em," Washington said.

"That was garbage," Alvo said. "Can't let a guy walk out in front like that without putting a body on him."

"What's with the short shift?" a woman called from the stands.

"Keep your goal scorers on the ice," a man said.

The voices sounded familiar. Rocket turned to look — Cash's parents were on their feet yelling at Alvo. They both wore Axmen sweaters.

Cash looked very unhappy as he came off. He gave Gold a pained look.

"Move over," he said to Rocket.

"We're before you," Bossy said.

"Hey, Jamie," Cash said to Gold. "Can we get back out there? I'll get it back."

Alvo leaned toward Washington's ear and spoke.

"Rockwood's line is next," Washington barked.

Gold went over and said something to Washington, who spoke to Alvo. Then Alvo shook his head and said something back.

"Rockwood's line is next," Washington said simply.

Gold's eyes narrowed and he stomped over to the far end of the bench, arms crossed.

The Breakaway had worked to perfection. Rocket figured another play was in order.

"As soon as we get a faceoff in their end, I'm going to knock the puck into the corner," he said to Bossy and Fryer. "The closest winger fires it behind the net to the opposite winger, and then we set up the cycle. Don't forget to look for the point shot."

This time he got a warmer reception.

"Makes sense to me," Bossy said.

"You got it," Fryer said.

Rocket felt like he could skate through a brick wall or jump over a building. One shift at a time, one goal at a time, and he would be a centre for the Axton Axmen. He could feel it.

CHAPTER 19

The speakers crackled, and then the song came back in clearly. Rocket licked his lips and sat up. The air in the bus was dry and he was dying for a drink, but the boys in the back had taken all the water bottles. There was no way he was going to ask for one.

He could never sleep on buses or trains, unlike Kyle, who'd conked out hours ago. He'd just leaned his head against the window and was gone. Most of the guys up front were sleeping. Even the guys in the back were fairly quiet now.

After the long trip there and back, the seats felt like concrete blocks. Of course, Rocket would travel another thousand kilometres to play a game like that again. He'd connected on a close in, one-timer feed from Fryer in the second for a goal. Then Fryer had put the game away with an empty-netter with a minute to go. They'd won 6–3, and his line had gotten four of the goals.

His hand hurt like crazy, though. He regretted not asking Chenny for some ice, but he still didn't want Gold or Alvo to know. He'd fire the beanbag up when he got home. That thing was a lifesaver. He owed Devin big time.

Alvo had sounded almost happy after the game. "Rocky start. We have to fix that," he'd said. "Second and third periods were okay — and I like how we buried our chances." That was it for the positive feedback. At least under Alvo you didn't have to worry about getting too full of yourself.

Rocket leaned his elbow on the armrest and put his chin in his hand. He smiled to himself, happy nobody had shaved his head. He'd been terrified when they got back on the bus, and he'd almost had a nervous breakdown when Kyle took a seat close to the middle. Rocket had wanted to sit with the coaches.

Nothing had happened. Cash, Hoffer and Gruny had been messing with him. All they did was chirp at guys and goof off, and now even that was done. Probably sleeping. Nothing like a hockey game and a fourteen-hour drive to calm guys down. Rocket pulled out his phone. Home in less than an hour. Megan and he had texted until she went to bed. Maddy had traded texts with him for a while, too. She was coming to Axton for tomorrow's game against the Knights.

He was worried about Maddy, so it would be good to see her. Tonight she'd admitted that Connor and Raja had hassled her the day before. She'd been with André, so they'd backed off, but today she hadn't gone out alone.

Rocket turned his phone off and stuffed it in his pocket. At least she'd have a chance to relax in Axton. Connor and Raja would likely lose interest if Rocket wasn't around. Their problem seemed to be with him.

At least, he hoped so.

He figured he'd take Maddy to Jimmy's, and they could hang with Kyle and Nathan.

Rocket looked out the window. The bus had just hit a construction zone and was crawling along. Maybe an hour was optimistic?

He closed his eyes. It felt good, even if he was still awake.

Suddenly, he was lifted out of his seat and pushed to the floor. He gasped for breath.

"Get the mouth," a voice whispered.

Hoffer?

A piece of tape stifled his cry for help. He tried to pull it off, but someone had pinned his arms. They rolled him onto his stomach and taped his hands behind his back.

"Mmmmmmm!" Rocket screamed.

A second, larger piece of tape covered his mouth entirely. He fought a wave of panic. He couldn't get enough air through his nose. They spun him to his back.

Akim looked down at Rocket from his seat, his eyes wide open.

"Transport the client to the hair salon."

Two guys began to giggle.

"Shhhhh," Hoffer hushed.

It was happening. They'd waited until everyone was asleep. Two hands hooked him under the armpits, and he was dragged to the back and tossed onto the seats in the last row.

No one could see him. He was done for.

Hoffer leaned forward on one knee, an evil grin on his face.

Rocket bent his own knee and kicked Hoffer in the chest. Hoffer flew back, and Rocket sat up. He needed to get back to the front so the coaches could see him.

"Not smart, Little Guy," Hoffer growled.

He pushed Rocket, slamming him into the window. Rocket lost his balance and slid into the space in front of the seat. For a crazy moment, he thought of trying to crawl under the seats. A hand grabbed his right ankle to end that notion, and another held his left. He heard the sound of duct tape ripping, and soon his ankles were taped together, too.

"You need to calm down," Hoffer said. He pulled Rocket back up and pushed him firmly onto the seat, flipping his legs up, too. Hoffer then sat on his legs. He reached over and pinched Rocket's nose. He couldn't breathe!

Rocket kept perfectly still and tried not to panic. He was helpless.

Hoffer let go. "Are you going to be trouble?" he asked.

Rocket shook his head. Not being able to breath had scared him. It felt like more was at stake here than his hair.

"Behave, Little Guy," Gruny said over Hoffer's shoulder. He snapped a pair of scissors open and shut a few times. "Be nice and we might let you keep your eyebrows."

"No chance. Eyebrows go," Cash said.

"Obviously," Gruny said. "I'm messing with him."

"Mmmmmmm," Rocket murmured. They were such jerks. He'd look like a total freak.

"Who wants the first snip?" Gruny said.

"I'll have a go." Cash took the scissors. "Welcome to the Axmen's Hair Salon. I'm the Cash-Man, and I'll be your stylist today. Do you want a shampoo? No? Fine. I understand you want a complete shave. Is that correct? I'll take that as a yes. Let's begin, shall we?" He grabbed a piece of Rocket's hair.

Gruny pulled a can of shaving cream and a razor out of his backpack.

"Okay, guys. Initiation is over."

Bossy! He was in the seat beside them.

"Bro, we just got started," Hoffer said.

"You got started plenty. That's enough," Bossy said.

"Go back to sleep," Gruny said. "We'll take care of this. He's a rookie."

"Do I have to get out of my seat?" Bossy said.

The three tormentors looked at each other.

Finally, Hoffer shrugged. "Way to kill it, Bossy. We're not allowed to have fun this year?"

"Untie him," Bossy said.

"You do it," Hoffer snapped.

Hoffer took hold of Rocket's shirt, pulled him to standing and then threw him onto Bossy's lap. Rocket's head banged into Fryer, who woke up with a start.

"What the . . . ? What are you . . ." Fryer stopped himself. "What's going on?" he said.

"Hoffer, Gruny and Cash were going to shave Little Guy," Bossy said.

"Is that so?" Fryer said slowly

Bossy stood Rocket up in the aisle and then stood up himself.

"This is going to hurt," Bossy said.

Rocket nodded. He didn't care as long as he could

breathe normally again. Bossy pulled the tape off his mouth. His cheeks and lips tingled painfully. He filled his lungs a few times. Air had never tasted so sweet.

"Turn around," Bossy said.

He took the tape off Rocket's wrists. It stung.

Rocket crouched down and began to untape his own ankles.

"Next person who messes with my centre, messes with me. Got it?" Bossy said.

"Next person who wakes me up will lose more than their hair. Got it?" Fryer added.

"Got it?" Bossy said again.

"Yeah. Whatever," Cash said.

Bossy took a step toward him. "You think you're serious stuff because you're Gold's pet? You've gotten a free pass till now, but you're pushing it way too far. Do you understand me?"

"Just joking around a bit. Geez," Cash said.

Bossy and Fryer turned back to Rocket.

"Thanks," Rocket said. That sounded a bit lame considering what they'd done. "I guess my hair and my eyebrows thank you, too," he added.

Bossy burst out laughing. "Like I said, no one messes with my centre."

"Well . . . thanks. I owe you guys."

"Just keep those sweet passes coming," Bossy said.

"You got it," Rocket said. "Um, so, I'll see ya."

He went back to his seat.

"You okay?" Akim said when he sat down.

"Yeah. No problem," Rocket said.

Kyle was still sleeping. He could sleep through anything, it seemed.

Akim leaned across the aisle. "Sorry," he said. "I didn't know what to do. I was going to tell the coaches, but . . . I'm sorry. I should've."

Akim didn't want to be a rat. Rocket got that.

"That would have just made it bad for you, too. Anyway, no big deal. They only wanted to scare me," Rocket said.

"I was scared enough for the both of us." Akim looked around and came over to Rocket's seat. "I'm going home," he said quietly. "They're going to pick on me, I know it. I don't have any friends and Glassy treats me like dirt. It's only a matter of time. I mean, they're picking on you, and you're an awesome player. They haven't done anything to me because they haven't noticed me. I doubt I'll even make the cut, anyway." He gripped the armrest. "I'm going home."

Kyle suddenly yawned and rubbed his eyes. "This drive is taking forever. You guys get any sleep?"

"I've been hanging with my bros at the back of the bus," Rocket said.

Akim laughed.

Bossy and Fryer came up to join them. "Hey, Little . . . Bryan, you okay for real?"

Rocket rubbed his upper lip. "I think I lost a few layers of skin, but I'll live."

"Layers of what?" Kyle said.

"Kyle's a heavy sleeper," Rocket joked.

"Did I sleep through something again? Story of my life," Kyle said.

"Hoffer, Gruny and Cash were being idiots, as usual," Bossy said. "They wanted to shave . . . Do I have this right, you're the Rocket?"

"My last name is Rockwood. Some guys call me that."

"Suits you. Anyway, they were going to shave Rocket," Bossy said.

"I owe you guys," Rocket said again.

Kyle cast an angry look toward the back of the bus. "Bro, I'm so sorry. I'm having a nap while you're fighting for your life."

"The tape around my mouth made it hard to call for help," Rocket said.

"Jerks," Kyle muttered.

"I figured they were just going to scare you," Bossy said. "We always do a little initiation to rookies, supposed to be fun. Maybe it isn't. I should've stepped in earlier."

"I don't get how Cash thinks he can pull this act off," Fryer said. "He's a rookie, too."

"Gold thinks he's the next OHL superstar," Bossy said.

"He sucked today," Fryer said. "Got schooled on that goal, the one Rocket's buddy got. Rocket, you got a goal and three assists, and I think you won every faceoff. You should be on the first line."

"Along with you guys," Rocket said, embarrassed by the attention.

"I just hope Alvo keeps letting us play," Bossy said.

"He will, and we'll do some real damage once we get used to playing with each other," Rocket said.

"I hope so. I'm done being the team goon," Bossy said. "Three years — I'm sick of it. Gold tells me fighting is my ticket to the NHL. He treats me like an attack dog: *Fight, Boss, fight. That's a good boy.*" He rubbed the knuckles on his right hand. "Kyle, is your buddy Nathan okay?"

"He's good," Kyle said.

"He stuck in there. Did well for himself," Fryer said.

"Gold told me to scrap because Nathan hit Cash. I shouldn't have done it. He seemed like a good guy," Bossy said.

"I appreciate that," Kyle said. "I'll tell him. You guys should come to Jimmy's sometime and hang with us."

"Definitely," Bossy said.

Fryer grinned and shadow-punched Bossy with a one-two combination. "So, when are you going to tell Gold and Alvo you're quitting the fight game?"

Bossy lowered his eyes. "Soon. Hockey has changed. Sure, you got to be tough, and sometimes you're going to drop the gloves to stick up for yourself or your teammates. I'm up for that. But I'm not going to be the guy who skates out for two shifts a game and drops his gloves like a trained monkey."

"Not even if they pay you three million a year?" Fryer laughed.

Bossy shook his head. "How many enforcers have to quit with concussions? How many guys get really sick from taking too many shots to the head? I don't even know how many fights I've been in, and I'm just twenty. Anyway," he went on. "I may not have skills like you, Rocket, but I'm big and I can play if they let me. I don't want to quit hockey, but I'm finished being a fighter."

"We work hard and figure out more plays off the cycle, you'll be in the NHL as a power forward. You both will," Rocket said. He could come up with a half-dozen plays off the top of his head.

"I like the sound of that. This season's off to a great start. We're scoring and getting ice time," Bossy said.

"I'm in," Fryer said. "I can play with this guy any day." He gave Rocket a punch in the arm.

"Anyway, you boys can relax on the initiation front," Bossy said. "That's done — or they deal with us."

"Bourquey's with us, too, I bet, and Rainer and Big Z," Fryer said. "We were talking about it after the game. Cashman had better smarten up, or he'll find himself without hair one day. I don't care how much Gold loves him. It's about respect for the game."

The boys all nodded. They joked around for another half hour. When the bus pulled into the parking lot of the Axton arena, Bossy and Fryer went back to their seats.

"Okay, boys," Gold called from the front. "Wake up. Collect your stuff. It's late and your billets are waiting to take you home." He clapped a few times. "We have a practice tomorrow at ten o'clock and don't think you can sleepwalk your way through it. It'll be full throttle. So everyone up and at 'em."

Akim looked at Rocket. "Maybe I will stay around a little longer and see if I make it."

He punched Kyle and Rocket's fists and returned to his seat.

"So they actually taped you up and were going to shave your head?" Kyle asked.

"Let's say I was getting worried about the eyebrows."

"The wacky life of an OHLer." Kyle grinned.

Rocket stuffed his sweatshirt into this backpack. He'd been in Axton for four days — it could have been four years. Wacky didn't go far enough.

CHAPTER 20

The bus rolled into the arena parking lot in front of a surprisingly large group of people.

"At the rink by nine-fifteen, and on the ice by ten," Gold said. "And don't forget your binders."

"What if we lost ours?" Cash called out.

Rocket headed to the door. He wasn't interested in Cash's humour.

As each boy stepped off the bus, the waiting crowd cheered and clapped.

"Yeah, Axmen."

"Go Axton, go!"

"Big win, boys. Big win."

Rocket laughed out loud. This was crazy, like they were in the NHL. It was after midnight, and there were at least fifty people to welcome them home. One guy caught his attention. He was dressed in black from head to toe — he even wore a black cowboy hat. He was talking to Cash's parents and Strohler.

Rocket pulled his hockey bag from under the bus.

"You can leave that," Chenny said. "I'll put it in the dressing room for tomorrow's practice."

"I can help," Rocket said. He looked for his sticks.

"It's fine. It's my job," she said.

"But . . ."

"Seriously, I need to do it." She shot a glance over Rocket's shoulder at Gold, grabbed two bags and wheeled them into the arena.

He felt bad about her having to do all the work. If the players helped, it would get done in five minutes. She sure seemed stressed. Maybe the pressure wasn't only on the players.

"Hi, Bryan," Devin said. "Awesome game!"

"How do you know already?"

"We listened on the radio," Devin said. "I kept the stats, as best I could — tough just listening. I had to guess a bit."

"Gotcha. Is your dad ready to go? I'm beat."

"I'd keep your distance," Devin said. "There's been a significant development in the Cash sweepstakes."

"What's up?"

Devin pointed at the guy with the cowboy hat. "Apparently, that's Robert Bickles. He's another agent. Dad's feeling the heat." Devin pressed his lips together. "Uh-oh, Dad-alert. Here he comes. Sorry," he whispered.

Strohler was storming toward them.

"Let's go," Strohler said harshly. "Why didn't you get him into the car, Devin? Can you do anything right? Apparently not. Ridiculous how late the bus is. I've got to work tomorrow."

"There was construction . . ."

"C'mon."

Strohler got in the car and slammed the door. He

drove away the second Rocket and Devin got in.

"Can't believe it. The garbage I put up with. It'll stink for a hundred years." Strohler was practically yelling. "Stupid liars, both of them. Such trash. Ungrateful pair of idiots. The hours I listened to their stupidity."

Devin pulled his headphones on. Rocket didn't dare move a muscle. The wheels squealed as they turned the corner sharply and accelerated down the street.

"What's this about your sister?" Strohler barked at Rocket.

"Yeah . . . my sister wants to see the home game tomorrow against the Knights, and . . ."

"I'm not a hotel, you know," Strohler said.

"Sorry. I asked Kimberly and she said it was okay."

"It's not okay," Strohler said.

He barrelled through two stop signs and pulled into the driveway. He was out of his seat in an instant and ran into the house. Rocket and Devin slowly followed him in.

"In front of my face! Right in front of me! Can you believe it?"

Strohler was screaming.

"Okay, Carl. Let's get Devin and Bryan off to bed and we can discuss it," Kimberly said. She smiled at them, but her face was flushed and she looked upset. "How was the game, Bryan?" she said.

"It was great. We won 6–3."

"Big deal," Strohler huffed. "They didn't have four of their starters, and their number one goalie didn't play. Knights will destroy you tomorrow."

"Okay, Carl," Kimberly said.

"Okay? Nothing is okay. I still can't believe Bickles showed up at the arena, at twelve-thirty in the morning, just to rub my nose in it. He's a snake, a snake in the grass. Acts like a huge big shot because he represents a few NHLers. I know a thing or two about him. He's a joke with the other agents. A huge joke. "

"I'm going downstairs," Devin said.

"Good solution, Dev. Game your brains out." Strohler glared at him.

Devin left.

"Carl, that's enough," Kimberly said.

She turned to Rocket. "Good night, Bryan. You must be tired — so much travelling for one game. Anyway, I'm off to bed, too."

"Okay, good night." Rocket turned and went downstairs. How awkward was that? If he made it, would he really be able to stand a year of Strohler?

Strohler began to yell again, but Kimberly cut him off: "I am so sick and tired of your juvenile behaviour!"

"Nice! I'm trying to deal with this Cash situation and here you are—"

"I don't care about Cash!" she said.

Devin came out of the movie room. His face was pale, but his eyes were cold and hard. He put a finger to his lips.

"Hold on, I just got a text," Strohler said. "Yeah! Perfect! Cash is signing with Bickles. With a stupid old man. After all I've done for them, I get a text!" He started on another tirade.

"Keep your voice down," Kimberly hissed. "The boys will hear."

"So what? That Bryan is gone. I'll see to that. Nice piece of work he did connecting me with Cash. Kid turned out to be useless."

"That's enough. Bryan's our guest and he's a great kid."

"When did you become Miss Congeniality?"

"This is done. I'm done!" Kimberly yelled.

Rocket was startled. She sounded so angry. Devin froze.

"You've been horrible ever since this hockey-agent obsession started. I'm not putting up with it any longer. You order Devin around and insult him and—"

"Obsession?" Strohler interrupted. "I'm trying to make a living here. I can't work for your oh-so wonderful father anymore. He operates the business like it's the 1950s. Barely knows what a computer is. I'm going to do things my way, and I'm going to be the biggest agent in the biz. I don't need Cashman. I have lots of other prospects, better ones — way better."

"Please just stop. You need to go," Kimberly said.

Rocket didn't know what to do. He shouldn't be listening to this, but he worried they'd hear him if he moved. Strohler would go crazy on him.

"Go where?" Strohler snapped.

"Away — a hotel."

"What? Why?"

"Because I can't be here with you any longer. Or I'll go, with Devin and Bryan. Make a choice. I'm done. I've tried. I've tried for so long. But this obsession has turned you into something unbearable. Why is it so important to become an agent? What do you have to prove? You didn't make the NHL. Let it go."

"I was cheated!" he screamed. "I should've been in the NHL. All those years I played, all those hours I practised. I played against guys who were half the player

I was and they made it. I should have made my millions—"

"Will you leave or should I get the boys and go?"

They were silent for a good minute.

"This is crazy. You're not going anywhere, and neither am I," Strohler said.

"You don't get to tell me what to do. That's over. Make your decision," Kimberly said.

"This is my house, too," he said. "I'm not going anywhere."

Devin ran past Rocket and up the stairs.

Rocket went to his bedroom, hoping he wouldn't hear anymore. But then Devin began shouting, and Rocket heard every word.

"Would you just get out of this house and leave us alone?" Devin yelled at his father.

"Devin . . ." Strohler seemed to be struggling for words. "We're a team. You and me. We . . . We're . . ."

"We aren't anything," Devin said. "All you do is tell me how useless I am. I may not be any good at hockey, but look what it's done to you."

"Kim . . ." Strohler tried again.

Again, they went silent.

"Really?" Strohler said. "That's what you both want? Okay, fine. Whatever. I'll prove you wrong, too. I'll prove everyone wrong. And don't think you can come running back to me when I'm the number one agent in hockey. This is your last chance."

Kimberly quietly said something, but Rocket couldn't make it out.

What was going on? He couldn't help himself. He opened the door a crack.

He heard the front door open and then close with a slam.

Rocket closed his own door and sat on his bed. Brutal for Kimberly and Devin. They were probably better off without Strohler, in his opinion, but still . . .

Rocket had been much younger than Devin when his own parents broke up. He remembered vaguely that they used to fight a lot, but that was it. One night they'd sat him down at the kitchen table. They'd told him Daddy was going to stay in another place for a while, but that they both loved him very much.

Rocket wasn't sure his dad loved him much at all.

A knock sounded at his door.

"Come in."

Devin poked his head in. "Sorry about that."

"It's okay. I guess your dad sort of thought he had Cash wrapped up," Rocket said.

He didn't know what else to say.

"My mom wanted me to apologize. Did you hear it all?" Devin asked quietly.

Rocket felt himself getting red in the face. "Did he leave?"

"Yup." Devin paused. "You know what? I used to really like hockey. Dad made me quit. Told me there was no point. I sucked too much to make the NHL." Devin shrugged and crossed his arms. "He wasn't always like this. We were a real family when I was a kid. Now all he thinks about is signing players and making millions of dollars. Does it look like we need more money?"

"Guess not."

Devin opened his mouth, as if to say something else, and then just leaned against the wall.

"My parents got divorced when I was a little kid," Rocket said. He hadn't meant to say it. It had just blurted out.

"Who do you live with now?"

"My mom."

"And your dad?"

"I don't see him too often." Rocket checked himself. "That doesn't mean that . . ."

"I get it. Who knows what will happen? I don't think my dad is going to change, though. I think he cares more about being an agent than me or my mom. I think that's just the way it is."

Rocket felt so badly for Devin, but he knew there was nothing he could do. Nothing he could say would make Devin feel any better about this. Sometimes in life you just had to experience things and get through them.

"I'm real sorry for what happened, Devin," Rocket said finally. "I'm sorry for your mom, too."

"Thanks." Devin looked at his phone. "It's late. See you tomorrow."

He closed the door behind him.

Rocket lay down on his bed. His eyes suddenly felt like they weighed a hundred pounds each. He should call Maddy and tell her not to come. What would happen tomorrow when he saw Cash, Hoffer and Gruny? He was going to be a zombie during practice . . .

His mind shut down as he drifted away.

CHAPTER 21

Honk! Honk!

Car tires squealed. A driver opened his window.

"You trying to kill yourself?" he yelled at Rocket.

Rocket skipped onto the sidewalk. He probably shouldn't have tried to gun it across the street like that. The car hadn't missed by much.

Kimberly had needed to open her store this morning, so she couldn't drive him. He didn't mind. The walk to the rink gave him a chance to clear his head.

The morning had been a bit crazy. He'd woken in a panic because he'd fallen asleep before telling Maddy not to come today. But he'd spoken to Kimberly about it, and she'd told him not to worry. She still wanted Maddy to stay.

He was happy with that. He missed talking to Maddy in person — not that he'd ever tell her, naturally!

Rocket checked the time on his phone. He was cutting it close, so he began to jog down the street. It felt good to stretch his legs.

As he got to the arena, a door popped open.

"Are you in a hurry to get somewhere?" Bossy was grinning.

Rocket wasn't going to get into the whole story. "My billet abandoned me and I had to walk."

"Relax, bro. We're the third line, now. We got to add some swagger to our game. Can't show up all panicked."

"Third line? Hope so," Rocket said.

"Come on. We're in room six, the small one. Not sure why. Something about cleaning. Like they couldn't have done that yesterday."

"Did you just get here, too?"

"Nah, I got here early. I wanted to have a chat with some of the vets — about last night. But then Gold came in, started going on about playing with passion, fighting for every puck, *blah, blah, blah*. I couldn't take it, so I said I needed to make a call. I saw him leave the room a minute ago."

They walked into the dressing room. Rocket looked around for his bag. He saw Kyle in the far corner and nodded hi.

Then he saw Cash watching him.

Great. Why did Chenny have to put his bag beside Cash's?

Rocket kept his gaze steady as he took his seat.

Cash smirked and nudged Hoffer. "He would've looked better with a haircut."

Hoffer and Gruny grinned.

Bossy and Fryer were watching intently, and so was Kyle. Rocket pushed his bag forward.

"Did your line get a point against the Knights? I can't remember," Rocket said.

"Scores a goal and he's a superstar," Cash said. "I had seventy-eight last year, so calm down, Little Guy."

"This isn't midget," Rainer said from across the room.

Cash seemed taken aback. "Yeah, I've sort of figured that out. I'm just saying . . ."

"Maybe a little less saying and a little more showing," Bourque said.

"Don't worry about me," Cash said.

"Mellow it out, bro," Hoffer said to Bourque. "Why you getting on him?"

"Why are you getting on my centre?" Bossy demanded.

"Are you making problems — over some rookie?" Gruny said.

Rocket had a feeling he should keep quiet. The vets had to work this out.

Rainer unzipped his bag slowly. "Do you want to have a problem with me?" he asked in a measured tone.

"Or me?" Bourque said.

"Or me?" Big Z said.

"No," Hoffer said carefully.

"You had one last night," Bossy said.

"We're still talking about that?" Gruny asked.

"We were just having fun," Cash said. "You think we were actually going to do it? You can be suspended for that."

"You don't do stuff like that without talking to the vets first," Bossy said. His eyes narrowed. "And don't touch Rocket."

"Give me a break," Cash said. "He's Little Guy. We can shorten it to LG if he wants."

"And you're Big Mouth — we can make it Shut Up, Big Mouth, if you want," Rocket told him.

Cash jumped to his feet and Rocket matched him. Cash lashed out, smacking Rocket's head with the heel of his hand. Rocket struck back with both hands to Cash's chest. Cash swung with his right. Rocket ducked, the blow grazing the top of his head. He sprang forward and crashed his shoulder into Cash's exposed ribs. Cash tripped over his bag and fell to the floor.

"Ah! You broke my shoulder," he screamed. He lay writhing on the floor. Rocket stepped back. All the guys crowded around.

"Get up," Rocket said. "You're such a faker — like when you skated into Nathan and acted like you'd been shot."

"My shoulder . . ." Cash rolled onto his knees holding his right elbow with his hand.

"I think you really messed him up," Gruny said.

"Deserved it," Fryer said.

He probably did, but Rocket's heart did a few flip-flops. This could be bad.

Bourque bent down. "You really hurt or is this more of your acting?"

"He broke my shoulder. Is that good enough for you?" Cash said. His face was twisted in pain.

Bourque and Glassy helped him sit on the bench. "Someone should get Chenny," Bourque said.

"Hang back, bro," Kyle whispered in Rocket's ear.

Rocket followed him to the far corner.

"Don't worry about it," Kyle said. "We all saw it. You were just defending yourself."

Rocket couldn't find the words. He could be in

serious trouble. A fifteenth-rounder didn't break a first-rounder's shoulder.

Chenny came running into the room with Washington.

She sat next to Cash and took his arm in her hands. "Can you move your arm at all?" she said.

"A little."

"How about your fingers?"

Cash wiggled them. Rocket watched intently. He hoped those were good signs.

"Where's the pain?"

"It's at the back. I fell on it. I think I hit the corner of the bench," Cash said.

"What happened?" Washington said.

"Rockwood jumped me, and I fell over my bag. Can't believe he broke it."

"I'm not sure it's broken," Chen said. She'd been pressing on his arm and shoulder the entire time. "I think it might be a bruise. Let me try and move it." She took his arm and gently moved his elbow away from his body. "I don't think we have any broken bones," she said.

"Let's have Dr. Hull look at him," Washington said.

Chen help'ed Cash up and walked him out the door.

"Rockwood — outside with you, too," Washington said.

"It wasn't like that," Rocket said.

"Outside," Washington said coldly.

"He didn't start it," Kyle said.

"I'm not talking to you right now," Washington said. He looked freaked out.

Rocket swallowed hard and headed out.

"You can wait for me in the stands," Washington said as he went by. "I need to talk to the guys."

Rocket watched the door close. His mind whirled as he made his way to the stands. He tried not to get too worried. The boys would tell Washington the truth about what went down — other than Hoffer and Gruny. But obviously this wasn't good. Gold and Alvo wouldn't be impressed with two teammates fighting. On the other hand, Cash was a huge baby. It was probably nothing.

Rocket leaned forward, elbows on his knees, chin in his hands. The ice glistened, the thin layer of water from the Zamboni still not dry. It was a beautiful sight: a fresh sheet, untouched, begging to be skated on. The desire to get dressed and skate almost overwhelmed him. He sat back. The arena was quiet, apart from a soft, high-pitched hum from the lights. Too quiet, really. He liked it better noisy, with people and pucks banging off boards and blades scratching the ice.

Time dragged on and on. How long did it take to find out that Cash had hit him and Rocket had body-checked him back? He thought about it. Did he really have to hit Cash back? He could've just moved away. And he should have kept his mouth shut in the first place. He'd probably only stood up to Cash because he felt he had support on the team — and maybe to prove he could take care of himself, too.

Rocket knew he'd have to fix this. Best way would be to apologize in front of the entire team, then shake hands with Cash, Hoffer and Gruny. Get it over with, accept whatever punishment came his way. Then get back to business — which was to make the team and win some games.

Rocket clasped his hands behind his head. The clock read ten. Practice was supposed to start.

"Hurry up, already," he sighed.

He heard footsteps and immediately sprang to his feet. Washington looked up at him.

"I know I shouldn't have reacted like that," Rocket blurted. "I lost it when he threw a punch at me — and maybe there's some history between us."

"You need to talk to Coach Alvo and Mr. Gold," Washington said. "They're waiting in the small meeting room."

"I lost my temper, but he threw the first punch. I shouldn't have pushed a teammate, though," Rocket said as they walked down the hall, passing Chenny. "Can you explain that to them, that I didn't mean to do it? That I'm sorry?"

"There's not much I can do," Washington said.

"But if you would tell them that . . ."

"I'm just the assistant coach," Washington said.

Rocket was stunned. Washington didn't seem at all interested in his side of things. Why wouldn't he help? He'd been the one to get Rocket drafted, and he'd voted to keep him after training camp.

Rocket turned back to Chen.

"Could you talk to them?" he asked her. His legs were shaky.

"I'm the trainer," she said in a sad voice. "I don't get involved in stuff like this. Dr. Hull took a quick look, though. Luckily he was here doing some paper- work. Anyway, Aaron has full range of motion. Like I said, it's probably just a bruise."

Rocket was so relieved, he could have cried. If

Cash's shoulder had actually been broken, Gold and Alvo would have lost it. Cash was fine. Rocket would tell them right off the bat that he was sorry and he was ready to apologize. They'd still be mad, but hopefully they'd be satisfied. It's not like Rocket and Cash were the first two teammates in history to have a fight. It happened all the time. Guys get competitive and something sets them off. Blowing off steam is what it was.

Washington opened the door to the room. Rocket went in. Alvo and Gold were sitting at the far end of a table.

"What did you do?" Gold thundered.

"I didn't . . . This is what happened . . ."

Gold slammed the table with his hand. Rocket nearly jumped out of his skin.

"This must be a joke," Gold said. "This midget attacks my best player and breaks his shoulder? We traded two guys, plus three draft picks to land Cashman and some nobody attacks him in the dressing room? Have I lost my mind? How did this happen?"

Alvo's smile was grim. "Maybe you can tell us what happened?" he said to Rocket.

"He threw the first punch. I didn't want to hurt him." Rocket's voice trembled. "I'm ready to apologize. He's a teammate, and I shouldn't have checked him."

"Why is this midget still talking?" Gold said to Alvo.

"The guys . . . Ask Kyle, Bossy, Bourque, Rainer, Big Z," Rocket said. "They'll tell you."

Gold reached for his phone. "This isn't going to work out. You're done."

Alvo looked up at Rocket, his eyes dull and the lines on his face deeper than usual.

Washington put his hand on Rocket's shoulder. Rocket shook it off.

"You can ask any of them," Rocket said. "I didn't start it. I didn't."

Gold swiped the screen. He wasn't listening.

"How about the fact that last night Cash, Hoffer and Gruny tried to shave my head? They tied me up with tape. I could barely breathe."

He could barely breathe now.

"We should go," Washington said. "Let's get your stuff."

"Honestly," Rocket said. "I was defending myself."

"I'm sorry," Alvo said.

Washington took Rocket by the arm. "We'll get your stuff. Come on."

Rocket couldn't see straight. Washington pulled him out the door. Everything was fuzzy.

"Do you want me to get your bag?" Washington asked.

Rocket shook his head. He had to do it.

No crying, Rockwood. Suck it up. End this like a hockey player.

He pushed the dressing room door open and went in. The guys were almost all dressed. A few were still taping their shin pads. Bossy was retaping his stick. Hoffer and Gruny were talking quietly together. Cash wasn't there.

"Hey, Rocket. What's up?" Bossy said.

Rocket got his bag and pulled out the handle. "Looks like this is it for me," he said.

Do not cry, he reminded himself.

Bossy's face fell. "What?"

"That's totally unfair!" Kyle said.

Rocket gave a weak laugh and shrugged his shoulders. "I don't think they were very interested in my side of the story. That's just the way it is."

Bossy came over. "This is plain wrong." He held out his hand.

Rocket looked at it. "Hope you don't mind, but I messed up my hand . . ." He held out his left fist instead, and Bossy gave it a bump.

Fryer came over and punched his hand, and then every other player on the team did, too, except for Hoffer and Gruny. Kyle was last. He looked really upset.

"Good luck with the season, boys," Rocket said. "In twenty years, I'll be bragging that I got to play with a bunch of NHLers. I'll be back to watch you guys play."

"Play Junior A this year and kill it. You'll be back next year, for sure," Bourque said.

"Nothing but a roadblock," Kyle said. "Get around it and keep going. You're the real deal — unlike some guys."

Hoffer and Gruny got up and left the room. The other boys said their goodbyes and filed out too.

Kyle held back for a minute. "Come by Jimmy's for lunch. We can talk about it. This is so brutal, it's not funny."

"My sister, or, I mean . . . My sister is coming. I have to meet her at twelve at the station. We can come by after."

"Awesome. See you then. You've got to check out the banquet burger. The bacon is wicked."

"Sounds good. Definitely."

Kyle left.

Rocket took a deep breath. Hockey dressing rooms didn't have the best smell, but it was sweet to him. He got his sticks and left.

Kyle, Bossy, Fryer, the others, they were good guys, but he knew they were hockey players first. Rocket wasn't on the team now. He'd be forgotten soon enough.

Washington was waiting for him. "Can I call your billet for a ride or should I call a taxi?"

They headed to the lobby.

"I can walk," Rocket said.

"Don't be silly. That's not right. I'll call a cab."

"Don't bother. It's ten minutes." He didn't want any favours from the Axmen.

Washington lowered his eyes. "I'm really sorry about this, Bryan. It's just that Gold thinks Aaron Cashman is going to be a dominant centre. He's a high draft pick, and guys like him sell tickets. He wasn't about to listen to me about what happened. If it makes you feel any better, the guys supported you. They said Cashman started it. But I can't go against Gold on this. He'd fire me on the spot."

"So the truth doesn't matter?" Rocket said.

"The truth isn't the point. The point is Gold's in charge, and what he says goes. I can't lose this job. I've spent years coaching minor league teams and travelling everywhere for tournaments. I have a little girl now. I have to make it as a coach. Like I said, Gold would fire me if I challenged him. Even Coach Alvo couldn't get him to change his mind."

"Coach Alvo was on my side?"

Washington looked surprised. "Coach Alvo has

always been your biggest supporter. He's the reason we drafted you. He put you on the line with Bossy and Fryer, and then with Nathan and Kyle. He's the one who insisted we keep you after training camp. He pleaded your case today, too, but like I said, Gold doesn't listen to anyone about anything." He shook his head and pushed open the door to the lobby. "He acts like he won ten Stanley Cups — single-handedly. I mean, sure he played in the NHL, but two years? Some superstar. Between you and me, I think Alvo's going to quit. I really do."

Rocket gripped his sticks together. Washington held his hand out.

"I'm sorry about this, Bryan. I am," Washington said.

"Good luck with your coaching career," Rocket said. "I'm sure you'll be great."

He walked off. Apology accepted, but he wasn't going to shake hands.

CHAPTER 22

Once again, Rocket's back was glued to the seat inside the bus station. There was no air conditioning in here, and it felt like he was in an oven. There was a breeze outside, but he didn't have the energy to move. He'd barely summoned the strength to get himself here.

The boulder was right back on his shoulders, twice as big as ever. Each time he thought about what had happened, he got more depressed.

One stupid moment, one dumb push and he was gone. What now? Where would he play? Should he just give up?

What about Maddy?

What about his mom?

What about when his mom found out he couldn't even get a NCAA scholarship now?

His back was on fire. He leaned forward and rested his elbows on his knees. Maddy should be arriving now. It was going to be so embarrassing. She may as well turn around and go home.

A bus pulled in, the brakes screeching as it came to a stop. Rocket got up and trudged over. How to even start? *Hi, Maddy. I pushed a guy and now my hockey career is over. Let's go back to our crappy apartment.*

The bus door opened and the passengers streamed out. He peered up into the windows to find her. He thought he saw a familiar face. Too short to be Maddy. He leaned against a metal pole and closed his eyes. He had a headache, a dull, throbbing pain. He never got headaches.

"Wake up, Mr. Tour Guide. We're here."

He opened his eyes.

"Megan?"

"You were expecting . . . ?"

"Maddy?"

"Two for the price of one," Megan said, as Maddy came up beside her. "And the rest of the gang is coming later, plus André, in about an hour. They couldn't get on this bus. No seats."

The ache in his head got worse. "I wish you'd told me you were all coming," Rocket said. "Besides, where are you going to stay?"

"My uncle and aunt live close by, in a big house. Lots of room," Megan said.

Maddy was eying him closely. "What's wrong, Bryan?"

He stared back at her. She could always tell.

Megan's smile disappeared. "Did something happen?"

He had to turn away. It hit him ten times harder than before. Kicked off the team for fighting — so embarrassing he wanted to scream.

He felt even worse for Maddy. This meant it was over. He'd let her down. His rep was toast. No OHL team would touch him. Now they'd never get out of that neighbourhood — or away from the Brigade.

"Let's go. I have some friends waiting at a restaurant. It's a couple of guys I know from the tryout and Devin, who I'm staying with. It's a cool place, and they're good guys."

Maddy crossed her arms. "Out with it, Rockwood. What did you do?"

"I didn't do anything."

She didn't move.

"Can we start walking?" he said. "This place smells like bus fumes."

"I could do without the fumes," Megan said.

They left the station and headed to Jimmy's.

"Bryan?" Maddy said.

"Okay. I did something. Maybe on the stupid side. The really, really stupid side." He rubbed his hands together. "It's a long story. The short version is there's this guy on the team . . ."

"You mean Cash?" Maddy asked.

He'd texted her about him. "Yeah. He and his friends tried . . ." They'd freak if he told them about the hazing. He decided to skip to today. "Anyway . . . I'm off the team, for fighting, not even for hockey. I got into it with Cash in the dressing room this morning. He was bugging me, as usual, and this time I burned him back, so he hit me. Then I pushed him, and he fell over a hockey bag and hit his shoulder. He wasn't really hurt, at least that's what the trainer told me, but Gold went ballistic and kicked me off the team. He's the owner and the general manager, so there was nothing anyone else could do. The coach tried, but . . ."

He balled his fists and bit down on his lip. The rage flowed through him. He was such an idiot.

"What about that Cash guy?" Megan said. "What happened to him?"

"Nothing. He's the golden boy, the first-round superstar. He does whatever he wants. Gold is in love with him. Like a total idiot, I go after him. How stupid can I be? I completely blew it. I was so close! I was getting ice time on the third line with two veterans. I could've made it. This could have been our chance, Maddy."

Maddy looked like she was about to say something, but Megan spoke first. "What are you going to do?"

"I don't know. This is really bad, way worse than when I got cut from the Huskies. Now I have a reputation for being a troublemaker. Another strike against me."

"I'm sorry, Bryan," Megan said. "I know how much this meant to you. For it to end like this . . ."

"C'mon," Maddy said. "This is where the Rocket gets his revenge and goes on to smoke the Axmen."

"This isn't a Disney movie," Rocket said. "I won't find another OHL team this season."

"Then next year," Maddy said.

"I need to think about it. This is so messed." He let himself laugh. He needed to. "Hey, I don't want to spend the rest of the day being depressed. Let's forget about it for now. I'll worry tomorrow." He shook his arms and body. "Done. Flushed. It's over. Move on. The Axmen are dead to me. No point thinking about it."

The girls remained oddly silent.

"It's probably time for me to focus on school and . . . I don't know . . . a normal life. Do you know the odds of making the NHL? It's like 3,000 to 1. Even if you make an OHL team, the odds are huge. Am I that good, a fifteenth-rounder with a bad rep?"

They didn't answer.

"Is it too late to call the guys and tell them not to come?" he asked.

"Yup," Megan said. "They're already on the bus."

He threw his hands in the air. "Perfect. Just unreal."

They turned the corner onto the main street. "There's Jimmy's. I'm having the three biggest banquet burgers of my life. Hopefully I'll explode and this will be all over."

"That sounds messy," Maddy said. "Could you at least blow up when we're not around?"

"I second that. It'd take forever to get the Bryan bits out of my hair," Megan said.

Rocket hadn't noticed before, but Megan's hair was different, thicker somehow, curlier. It looked nice.

"Okay, I promise not to explode anywhere near you. I'll go off by myself in a corner. I'll be the boy crying."

"You're always the boy crying," Maddy said.

"Stop trying to cheer me up."

Megan was texting. "I'll let the guys know to meet us here."

"I think I see Kyle and Nathan on the patio." Rocket opened the gate and walked over to the corner. "Hey, guys. Don't tell me you ate already."

"Only breakfast and a post-breakfast snack," Kyle said.

"And a pre-lunch nibble," Nathan added.

"Kyle, Nathan, this is Maddy. She's like my sister. And this is Megan . . . a friend."

Kyle and Nathan gave him a look.

"Hi, sister-like Maddy. Hi, friend-Megan," Kyle said.

"Maybe I didn't nail the intro," Rocket said.

"I live with Rocket and his mom," Maddy said. "So we kind of think of ourselves as related, but we're not."

"That must be a relief for you," Kyle said.

Everyone burst out laughing, Rocket most of all. Nathan was the first to stop.

"Kyle filled me in, Rocket," he said. "That was so wrong. I wish Kyle wasn't playing for them. It'll be the worst dressing room ever."

"Have a seat, ladies," Kyle said. "Welcome to Jimmy's. If you don't have the fries, you'll hate yourself forever. We can have wings, but we'll have to order the baby chicken fingers with sweet sauce for Rocket."

"I'm not good with spicy," Rocket said to Megan.

"Has Rocket told you about the fight?" Nathan asked the girls.

"Some fight," Rocket said. "I gave him a push."

"It wasn't the softest push I've ever seen." Kyle grinned.

"He told us a bit," Megan said.

"Can we not talk about it?" Rocket pleaded. "At least not until I stuff home a banquet burger?"

"Good call, young man," Kyle said. "You need some bacon grease in your system."

"I don't know what I need," Rocket said. Whatever he'd found funny about today suddenly vanished. "This is bad. I keep trying to be positive, to believe that I can get past this, but it's like what you said, Nathan. It's probably time to accept the facts. Hockey doesn't want me."

"I don't know if I agree," Nathan said. "You're the real deal. I'm not you. I can deal with that. It wasn't meant to be for me, but I don't think that's true for you."

"No way you're quitting," Kyle said. "That would be even worse than Cash getting away with another fake injury."

"Did he do this before?" Maddy asked.

Kyle clapped Nathan on the back. "This is victim number one. Cash ran into Nathan and acted like he'd been attacked by a pack of wild gorillas." Kyle put both hands out on the table. "Stop. Don't make a sound. I want to enjoy that image for a while. Hmm, wild gorillas attacking Cash . . ." A dreamy look crossed his face.

"Are you guys going to eat something . . . else?" Caroline was standing there, holding a pad of paper and a pen.

"We need a banquet burger for my slightly depressed friend, who isn't going to give up playing hockey," Kyle said. "What do the rest of you want?"

"Can I see a menu?" Megan asked.

Kyle and Nathan began laughing.

"You can't use a menu at Jimmy's. You got to feel it," Kyle said. "What hits you: burgers, wings, pizza, turkey club, ribs?"

"What about the fries?" Maddy asked.

"Fries are automatic. They come no matter what," Nathan said.

"How are the suicide wings?" Megan said.

"Am I the only wuss here?" Rocket asked, and then he put a hand across Maddy's mouth. "Don't answer that, please."

"We'll go with two pounds of suicide, and maybe a few hot wings as an appetizer," Nathan said. "And two baskets of fries, along with a plate of deep-fried cheese strings."

"I'll have the large salad with a baked chicken breast and some whole wheat bread," Kyle said.

They all turned to him.

"Sorry. I have a game tonight."

They all started laughing again. Even Rocket.

CHAPTER 23

"Okay, enough fooling around. Let's get serious." Kyle held a suicide chicken wing out to Rocket. "You aren't afraid of a teeny-weeny chicken wing, are you? It isn't going to bite you."

Devin was laughing away. Rocket was happy to see him having a good time, but less glad about the wing. They were all getting in on it. It was weird — even though most of them had just met, it felt like they'd been friends for years.

"Can't we just agree that I'm a total baby and leave it at that?" Rocket said.

"I can agree that Bryan's a baby," Maddy said.

"Thanks, Mads. Always there for me, as usual," Rocket said.

"I think you're a baby, too," Megan said.

"Me, too."

"I'm good with that."

"I'll make it unanimous," Kyle said. "But this isn't just any wing. It's The Wing."

"Ooooh," the others crooned.

"You eat this wing to show that you're not afraid of

anything — especially Gold and Cash. To show that you're going to battle through this and get back to the OHL. To show the Axmen that they messed up big time!" Kyle said.

"All hail The Wing," Nathan said, bowing to it.

Rocket took the wing from Kyle. "You were sort of holding it with your fingers."

"Ten-second rule."

"You were holding it for, like, a minute."

"Sixty-second rule."

Rocket took a deep breath.

"Rocket, no one's saying you have to knock your head against a brick wall forever," Maddy said. "One more year, give yourself one more kick at it, and then you'll know. If it doesn't work out, then no regrets. Do you want to second-guess yourself for the rest of your life?"

As usual, Maddy had known what he was thinking.

Rocket bit into The Wing.

His friends let out a cheer.

"Brutal," he gasped, trying to chew it.

"Go Bryan Go!" Maddy chanted.

"Water," Rocket cried.

"No cheating. Eat The Wing," Kyle said. "No aids."

Rocket figured he just needed to get it done. He pulled the rest of the meat off with one bite and some-how choked it down.

Megan slid some lemon slices over. "Lemons are better than water," she said. "The juice helps neutralize the alkaline spices."

Rocket wouldn't question Megan on science. He bit into a slice.

"So good," Rocket said. The burn melted away. "I never thought I'd love the taste of a plain lemon."

Kyle patted Rocket on the back. "I'm proud of you, bro, even though I still think you're a baby."

"Me, too," Maddy said. Then her face lit up and she raised her hand. "There's André."

André waved back and came over with Bird and Nigel.

"Hi, guys," Rocket said, feeling awkward. "I've got some good news and some bad news." He was going to have to tell the whole story again.

"Let's get another table," Kyle said, getting up. "I'm Kyle, by the way."

Rocket introduced everyone else as they pulled a table and some chairs over.

"So, give us the bad news first," Bird said. "Then you can cheer us up with the good news."

"Did you get hurt?" André said to Rocket. "Don't tell me you can't play tonight. We already bought the tickets." He pulled them out of his pocket and fanned them like a hand of cards.

"The bad news is, well . . . It's a long story." Rocket put his hands on his thighs and laughed. The whole thing was still hard to believe. "There's this guy named Aaron Cashman and . . ."

For the next fifteen minutes, he told them the story. "And now I'm sitting at Jimmy's, a suicide wing burning a hole in my stomach, with awesome old friends and awesome new ones. So things aren't that bad. I'm not quitting, not yet anyway, so I guess that's the good news."

"That's the craziest story I've ever heard," Nigel

said. "This Cash guy must be a king-sized jerk."

"He's not that big, but he's got the jerk part down pat," Nathan said.

Just then, Jimmy walked up to the table, laughing. "I think some of you know this man," he said.

Rocket was shocked to see Coach Alvo standing there. Even more surprising, Alvo greeted them with a big smile — it was strange to see him without his usual scowl.

"Greetings, everyone. Kyle, Nathan, Bryan, good to see you," Alvo said.

"Hi, Coach," the three of them said at once.

"I wonder if I might have a word with you, Bryan. Maybe back in the restaurant?" Alvo said.

"Sure, Coach." Rocket followed Alvo inside, casting a quick glance back at his friends. They seemed as surprised as he was.

"What can I get ya?" Jimmy asked Alvo as they sat down.

"Just an ice water please."

"Bryan?" Jimmy asked.

"I'm fine . . . Water maybe."

Jimmy went to the bar.

"I imagine you're wondering what's going on," Alvo said.

"A little."

Alvo grunted. "Maybe more than a little?"

"I guess." Rocket didn't know what to think.

"I can't imagine how difficult today has been for you. Not that this makes it any better, but it's been one of the more difficult days of my adult life as well. A couple of years ago the Axmen were sold to a new ownership group, and they brought in Jamie Gold. He'd convinced the owners he was up on the new statistical revolution and he could produce a winner. I pointed out that Axton was already a winner." Alvo made a sour face and waved his hand. "Anyway, that doesn't matter. What does matter is that since Gold became our GM, we've missed the playoffs two years in a row."

"Here are your two waters," Jimmy said, placing them on the table. He went off to serve another customer.

Rocket looked at Alvo. "Did you say the Axmen have owners, as in more than one?"

"Gold likes to think he's in charge," Alvo said. "The reality is he only owns a very small percentage of the team. The Axmen have three other owners, and they control things."

Alvo leaned his elbows on the table. "So that's why I'm here. I'd like you to come back to the Axmen. I first saw you play, believe it or not, back in bantam. I was there to scout some AAA players, and you were playing the game before. I think you were in AA?"

"I was with the Bowmont Blues," Rocket said.

Alvo laughed. "I'll take your word for it. Anyway, you caught my eye, and I've followed you ever since. Gold can't see past size and fighting." He shook his head. "He has no idea how much hockey has changed. Anyway, before the draft I made a big deal of wanting to make the last pick, like it was a joke. I figured if you went before, then it would be great for you. If you didn't, then it would be my lucky day. I was thrilled when you were available. You have the potential to be that exceptional player who makes a real difference."

"That's . . . nice of you to say," Rocket said, a little overcome. "Size is still a problem, maybe . . ."

"We'll know in a couple of years," Alvo said. "You never know with kids. Some grow in their twenties. All I know is you can help this hockey club. With Bossy and Fryer on the wings, you three make a dynamic line. I've always thought Bossy had more to his game than fighting. Gold wouldn't let him develop. Same with Fryer."

"What about Mr. Gold? Does he want me back?"

Alvo smiled grimly. "Like I said, Mr. Gold is not as powerful as he thinks. He interfered one too many times, and we've lost one too many games. After practice I made a phone call to the owners. I told them either Gold goes or I walk. Five minutes later, Gold was fired. Felt like a thousand pounds lifted off my shoulders, like I was free again."

Rocket took a sip of water.

"And the first thing I want to do as a free man is get a certain Bryan Rockwood back in the lineup."

"Wow. I mean, this is . . . This is a weird day. What will the guys thinks, though? And Cash?"

Alvo put on his hat. "That's my job. I'll do the coaching. You keep playing the way you've been so far."

"That's amazing. Thanks! This is awesome. I was just talking to my friends about finding a Junior A team and trying to make it back to the OHL next season, and . . ." He stopped. "Sorry, I know I haven't made the team yet."

"Keep playing like you have been, and you won't have any problem in that regard," Alvo said. "I've got you pencilled in as my third-line centre. Don't worry about Cash, or his linemates. If they give you a hard time, come see me and I'll stop it."

"I think Bossy, Fryer and some of the other vets will take care of that, Coach." Rocket grinned.

"Glad to hear it," Alvo said. "You've got a game tonight. I hope you didn't eat too many wings."

"I only had one," Rocket said.

No need for him to know about the banquet burger.

"Good to hear. Just don't tell me what else you ate," Alvo said.

Rocket had to laugh.

"Game's at eight. Be there at six. We have a pre-game skate at seven," Alvo said.

"This is . . . Wow! I don't know what to say."

Alvo held his hand out. Rocket shook it warmly, despite the twinge of pain.

"Glad to have you back," Alvo said as he got up. "Do your friends need tickets tonight?"

"I think they already have them."

"I'll see you later, then."

At the mention of his friends, Rocket thought of Nathan. "Coach, could I ask you about something? Did Gold cut Nathan because he ran into Cash? Because Nathan didn't mean to. Honest. Cash had his head down."

"I cut Nathan," Alvo said. "It wasn't Gold. I felt terrible about the fight. Gold lost it and ordered Bossy out there. Bossy was over the boards before I could stop him."

Alvo sat back down. "As for Nathan, I've known him for years — his father and I go way back. Nathan is a good player, but he doesn't have the tools. He might catch on with a Junior A team, or maybe even the right OHL team, but it won't go beyond that. He doesn't have the foot speed, and he doesn't have the size to offset that. He has that shot, and he can score, but he won't at the higher levels, at least not in my opinion. He was helped in camp by a great centre who set him up, and Kyle created a lot of opportunities for him, too."

Alvo took a sip of water, then continued. "There comes a time for most players when they have to accept their NHL dreams are over. I've been an OHL coach for almost twenty years. I've seen a lot of boys realize they won't make it; it's one of the hardest parts of this job. The prize is huge — it's impossible for some people to accept. But I think Nathan will be okay."

Rocket thought of Strohler.

"Thanks, Coach. It's none of my business, I know. I just wanted to ask."

"I appreciate a friend looking out for his buddy. See you later." Alvo grinned getting up again. "And I hope that wing doesn't slow you down."

He headed to the door. "Take care, Jimmy. See you at the game," he called out.

Jimmy waved and flashed a thumbs-up.

Rocket didn't move. He stared off in the distance, a thousand thoughts swirling through his mind. He felt like a yo-yo spinning up and down, out of control. The coach likes you and you play; the GM hates you and you walk. Was hockey nothing more than that — who you knew or just plain luck? He rubbed his stomach. The burger and the wing hadn't been the best pregame meal. He'd have to work that off.

"So, what happened?" Maddy said from behind.

He turned around. His friends were all around him.

Rocket sighed and held his hands up. "I'm back. Gold's fired. Go figure."

The boys basically attacked him. Maddy and Megan gave him big hugs.

"It was The Wing," Kyle said finally. "The power of the sauce came through."

"I'm worried about the sauce coming through me," Rocket said.

"Uck," Maddy said. "Disgusting boy-moment."

"Sorry — thought I was in the dressing room for a sec."

Kyle reached out his fist. "Awesome news, bro. It'll be good to see you in the room. The boys will be stoked."

"Not all of them," Rocket said pointedly.

"The ones that count," Kyle said.

"So what did he say exactly," Megan said, "and how did Gold get fired?"

They crowded around as Rocket began to tell the story.

CHAPTER 24

Rocket's nerves were on edge as he pulled his hockey bag into the arena.

"Don't forget, number 11 tends to give up the puck under pressure," Devin said. "He's their right defence-man. You could also exploit number 3. His foot speed could be better, and you can get the corner on him if he's not positioned. But he likes to hit. He had 182 hits last year."

Devin had been pounding him with stats about the London Knights ever since they'd returned home to retrieve Rocket's hockey equipment.

"Just remember the right skate goes on the right foot," Maddy said.

"How does that help?" Rocket said. "How am I supposed to play with one skate?"

"Ask your coach," Maddy said.

They stopped in the middle of the lobby.

"I got to admit, I'm a little nervous all of a sudden," Rocket said. He flexed his fingers. "I have this hand that's bugging me, I'm still short, and . . ."

Megan ripped his hockey sticks from his hand. "I

didn't come all the way to Axton to hear you doubt yourself. I came because this is important to you and you can do it. You've excelled at every level, and you're good. You have to believe in yourself. Put all your doubts aside and go for it. I don't care what the odds are. It's not about the odds. It's about digging deep, and . . ."

Rocket and Maddy stared at each other in disbelief, and then they burst out laughing.

"What? I'm trying to inspire you," Megan said. She began to laugh as well.

"You did," he said. He gave her a hug. "Thanks. You're right. Forget the odds. Forget this hand. Forget Cash. Forget everything. Just play hockey." He took his sticks back.

"Now I'm inspired," Bird said. "Where's the concession stand? I need a ten-year-old hotdog."

"I smell something disgusting over there," André said. "Follow me."

André led Bird, Devin and Nigel around the corner.

"I have a weakness for chocolate-covered raisins," Megan said. "I'll be back in a sec."

Rocket looked at Maddy warily. "You're not eating? Is the world coming to an end?" he said.

"I wanted to talk to you, when the others weren't around." She twisted her hair with her fingers.

"So, what's the deal, sis?"

She jabbed her finger into his chest.

"You need to stop thinking you have to take care of me and your mom. We aren't your responsibility. You're not a loser if you don't make this team. You're not a loser if you don't make the NHL. Go for it. You might do it. But you can't be so hard on yourself. Your mom and I don't worry about you making the Axmen. We worry about you putting so much pressure on yourself. And we worry that if you don't make it, you'll spend the rest of your life bitter about it."

Rocket put a hand on her shoulder. "But I have to make it. Mom's spent a fortune on my hockey, money she didn't really have, and how can she pay for you to go to university? You'll spend your life paying back student loans. And she deserves better than that crummy apartment. If I make it, we can finally get out of there, and I can pay for your school and . . . It solves everything."

Maddy poked him in the chest again. "Well, surprise, we are out of that crummy apartment. Or we will be soon. Your mom found a place. It's not great; it's in a basement. But it has three bedrooms and it's fairly big. It's close to school, so it's in a nice neighbourhood and I won't need to take the bus anymore."

Rocket couldn't contain his smile. "Really? Goodbye Mr. Connor and Mr. Raja?"

"I'm going to miss those two lugs," she joked. But she quickly turned serious again. "I'll figure university out and get on with things. I'm not giving up — ever — and neither are you. Promise me that. And promise me you'll stop trying to save me from some terrible fate."

"But Maddy—"

"What I can't deal with is you thinking I made your life harder. I can't," she said. "I don't know where I'd be if it weren't for you and your mom — living on the streets maybe."

"Never!"

"No mom or dad? No one who really cares about me? I'd even thought about it before you guys took me in."

"We're a family now, the three of us," Rocket said. "That's the way it is. Families take care of each other. I'm going to take care of you guys by playing hockey. That's my best shot. It makes sense."

"It makes sense if you play because you can and you want to, not because you have to," she said. "If you feel like there's some huge weight on your shoulders, it'll crush you eventually. Let it go. We'll be okay no matter what."

He thought about that boulder. He'd love to push it off, but he wasn't sure he could. He needed to think about it some more. The boulder would stay for now.

"Thanks for coming up, sis," he said.

"Thanks for dedicating your first goal to me," Maddy said.

"That's a deal."

"And you have to dedicate your second to Megan," she said.

"Um . . . okay."

"Because she's a good friend of yours, and it would make her very happy."

"Okay. Two goals. Got it. Anything else?"

"You could compliment her on her new hairstyle and clothes, too," she said. "Don't be so oblivious."

"Oblivious to what?"

Maddy raised her eyes to the ceiling. "That you guys have a connection. That she likes you. And it has nothing to do with trivia."

He had noticed, of course. But with so much going on in his life, and him moving to Axton to play, he'd decided to let it go. Megan and he were just friends. At least for now.

"Thanks for the advice," he said. "Say hi to André for me."

"Just don't trip over the blue line," she shot back as he headed toward the dressing room.

He pushed the door open.

"Yo, Bourquey, can you toss me some tape?" Rainer said.

Bourque threw over a roll of white sock tape.

"These boys are going to be stomping mad after we beat them in their own rink," Fryer said.

"Doesn't matter that this is an exhibition game," Bossy said. "We play this one hard."

Rocket put his sticks in the rack and walked further into the room.

"Thanks, Mr. Bourque. You're a gentleman and a scholar," Rainer said, tossing the tape back.

"Toss it here," Big Z said.

"Can I tape my own shin pads first?" Bourque grinned.

Rocket stood by the door, bewildered. No one even noticed he was there.

Then the corners of Bossy's mouth turned up just slightly. He put his head down. He was laughing.

"Okay. I fell for it. Proud of yourselves?" Rocket said.

The room erupted in cheers.

"Good to see you back," Bourque said. He clapped Rocket on the shoulder.

Bossy pulled Rocket's bag over to where he and

Fryer were sitting. "Got to keep the line together," he said.

Big Z nodded and said, "Hey." It was a long speech from the quiet defenceman, but it meant a lot.

To his right, Rocket saw Cash, Hoffer and Gruny huddled in the corner, talking in whispers.

Rocket reached for the zipper of his hockey bag, then stopped. He needed to do something, for the team, to set things straight. If it worked, awesome. If not, then he'd done what he could.

He went over to Cash and his friends.

"Guys, we haven't exactly gotten along. No point blaming anyone. Training camp is like that."

The three boys stared up at him.

"I'm sorry for shoving you this morning, Cash. I lost my temper. Teammates shouldn't do that. That's not the way I play, and that's not the kind of teammate I want to be."

Rocket stepped back and waited.

"Yeah, well, forget about it," Cash said quietly. "It's over. I deserved some of it, too. Sorry for taking that swing at you — and for the bus . . ." His voice trailed off.

Rocket had heard better apologies, but he figured that was big for Cash. As for Hoffer and Gruny, maybe they'd take longer to come around. Maybe they never would. So what? He was here to win games, not friends.

"Cool. Let's kick those Knights back to London," Rocket said.

He sat back down and unzipped his bag.

Big Z gave him another approving nod. Rainer flashed a thumbs-up. Rocket knew he'd done the right thing. He didn't like those three, but they were good players and they'd help them win — and they were Axmen.

Kyle walked into the room, and a big grin spread across his face.

"Something smells different," he said, sniffing the air.

"Are you saying I've got to clean my equipment?" Rocket asked.

Kyle came over and bumped fists with him.

"You should *definitely* do that. But I meant I can't smell any gold around here," Kyle said.

"Does gold smell?" Rainer said.

"Sometimes," Kyle said, and the room erupted in laughter. "Did the Knights even bother coming? They obviously have no chance," he continued.

"I like the confidence," Bourque said. "I bet they ice all their starters this time. It'll be a different team. We're going to have to battle."

"We got to shut down that Tyler Hopkins kid," Rainer said. "He killed us last game."

"That's the guy you know, right?" Bourque said to Rocket.

"You can't shut him down," Rocket said. "You've got to be on him when he doesn't have the puck. You can't give him any room. Otherwise, he'll start dipsy-doodling you to death and dish the puck around. You've got to play him straight up and hard."

"Hey, Cash. You hearing this?" Rainer said. "You have the size and speed to match up against that guy. You can do it. You up for it?"

Cash raised his gaze. He didn't look like the same guy to Rocket. The cocky grin was gone. Now he looked like any other sixteen-year-old kid trying to make it in the OHL.

"I'm ready. That dude ain't gonna touch the puck today," Cash said.

"Let's get ready, boys," Bourque said. "We want a good pregame skate, no messing around."

The room got quiet, apart from the sound of hockey tape whirling around sticks and shin pads.

Bossy elbowed Rocket. He leaned closer.

"Rumour has it Alvo went at Cash and his linemates for an hour," Bossy said in a hushed tone. "Bourque heard him. Alvo said he'd stick their butts to the bench for the rest of the season if they didn't change their attitudes. Then he said they'd have to earn back their ice time. They're on the fourth line until they prove themselves."

"Really? Well, Bourquey's line can step it up," Rocket said. "No problem."

Bossy's eyes twinkled. "Coach said he wants us to be the first line — an experiment."

Rocket taped up his shin pads. "Then we've got to go for it every shift. I don't know about you guys, but after what happened today, I'm not taking anything for granted. I can't. I got a lot riding on this." He thought about what Maddy had said, but that boulder was right where it had always been. He needed to make it.

"I've been thinking of a play," Rocket said to Bossy and Fryer. "It's not in the binder. It's a variation for the power play. Imagine the puck is in the right corner. Fryer brings it up the boards to the hash marks . . ."

He held out his hand to draw the play for them. His linemates leaned in close to see.

CHAPTER 25

The puck ringed the side wall. The Knights' right defenceman stretched for it. Rocket was a hair faster, knifing it out of the Axmen's zone off the boards. He avoided the defender's hip check and kept skating, veering into the middle of the ice.

"On it," Bossy yelled. He swooped in to corral the rolling puck. Then he and Rocket stormed in on the Knights' left defenceman on a two-on-one. The Axton fans were on their feet, screaming for a goal to break the third-period tie. The few London fans were rooting equally hard for the Knights to block it.

Bossy skated down the left side, the defenceman watching warily. The goalie had come out a good three metres from his line. Bossy faked a pass, took another stride and then fed Rocket on the right. The defender hesitated ever so slightly. Rocket didn't hesitate at all. He powered to the net on the right side. The defenceman pivoted on his left foot and extended his stick. The goalie slid over, squared for the shot. Rocket flew past the defender's stick, puck on his backhand. He lowered his shoulder as if to shoot, and the goalie dropped into his butterfly. Rocket immediately carved wildly on his inside edges, pulling the puck wide right. The goalie fell back and reached out with his glove hand. Rocket felt his balance go. At the last second, he backhanded the puck into the crease.

Rocket's feet went out from under him. He braced himself for the impact.

"Ooof."

The crowd roared. Rocket looked up. The puck was buried in the back of the net, and Bossy was holding his stick above his head.

Rocket turned his attention to himself. He prayed he hadn't wrecked anything.

"The Rocket comes through again," Fryer said from behind. He pulled Rocket to his feet.

Rocket would have preferred to remain on the ice until he was sure he was okay. But this worked. Nothing damaged. Even more important, it was 3–2 for the Axmen.

Bossy threw his arms across their shoulders.

"Ax-Attack, boys. Let's get greedy," Bossy said gleefully.

They broke up their huddle.

"Nice breakout," Rainer said, patting Bossy and Rocket on the helmet.

Big Z gave them all a healthy smack on the pads.

Rocket rested his stick across his knees. The boys on the bench were on their feet, but no one was coming on. Rocket followed Bossy and Fryer and slapped everyone's gloves.

"One more, Axmen," Kyle said. "Let's not get lazy."

Kyle had taken a regular shift on Bourque's line, and he'd been playing a great two-way game. Rocket could sense the other guys were treating him differently now — with respect.

Rocket glided to the dot, hunched over, head down. A chant of *Go Axmen Go!* swept the arena. Ty came out with his line.

Rocket had expected Alvo to bring Cash's line out — Cash had been going up against Ty most of the time and had done a good job. Ty's line had had its chances but hadn't connected yet. Alvo obviously wanted to see how Rocket's line would match up.

"Stop showing me up," Ty said to him. "Coach just told me to play more like you."

"You can't play like me. You suck too much. I'd probably quit hockey if I were you," Rocket said.

"I'll give myself one more shift, and then maybe," Ty said.

Rocket tapped Ty's shin pads with his stick. He didn't care what people thought. Once the puck dropped friendship was forgotten, and they'd tear into each other. But for now, the puck was in the referee's hands, and Rocket wanted to show Ty some respect. They'd been friends since they were nine.

The organ began to play and the fans clapped to the beat. The referee lowered his hand. Rocket and Ty had spent hours in Ty's basement practising draws. They knew each other's moves by heart. No point trying anything fancy. Rocket straightened up.

"Let's go, Axmen," he said loudly.

That was the signal. Bossy inched forward.

The referee blew his whistle and held the puck out.

Rocket and Ty put their sticks down. Rocket tensed his muscles. This was going to hurt his hand. The puck dropped. Ty tried to pull the puck back with a reverse-hand sweep. Rocket thrust his stick forward to block him. The impact sent a shockwave up the stick into his hand. He ignored the pain and held firm, swinging his left hip into Ty.

Bossy cut over, dug the puck from their skates and slid it back to Rainer.

"If you're going to cheat . . ." Ty said, giving Rocket a bit of a cross-check on the arm. Not hard, just enough to say it was time to play.

Rocket grinned and did a loop to the right to gain momentum. Rainer hit him in mid-stride. The Knights' left winger charged. Rocket shovelled a pass to Fryer and then swerved wider to avoid the check. The winger got a piece of him, but not enough to hold him up. Bossy had angled into the middle of the neutral zone, and he accepted a pass from Fryer. Ty showed why he was so good. He'd anticipated the play and got a stick on it, deflecting the puck to his left defenceman. The puck rifled across the ice to the right defenceman, and then up to the winger.

Big Z was a rock on defence. No way the winger could beat him one-on-one. Instead of pressuring the winger, Rocket hustled to get back to the corner for what he figured would be a dump-in. The winger seemed to accept that as well, and once he got close to the blue line, he lofted the puck into the corner. Big Z had to let him go or he'd get an interference penalty. Rocket had a step on the winger, however. The puck rested a few metres from the net, up against the boards.

Glassy wasn't able to play it. It was up to Rocket.

He could feel the winger closing in. Rocket had to make a split-second decision. Late in the third, up one goal, this wasn't the time to get fancy. He lowered his shoulder and curled hard on his edges, sending the puck behind the net with his backhand. The second the puck left his stick, the winger pounded him. Rocket's sideways momentum let him avoid most of the impact.

Rainer had the puck on his stick. He passed it to Bossy, up the middle, for an easy breakout. Rocket rounded the net and hustled to catch up.

"Awesome play, Rocket," Glassy called out.

Bossy got over centre and then banged the puck in deep, peeling off for a change. Rocket cut his own charge off at the blue line and came off as well. Cash's line came over the boards. On the bench, Alvo high-fived Bossy, Fryer and Rocket.

"I need to see you play with patience," Alvo said to the guys on the bench. "This isn't the time for goals. We have to finish this off, a complete game, both ends. Look for your chances and score if you can, but not at the expense of an odd-man rush. We need to learn how to play in a tight game with a lead. Rocket, that's the perfect play in our end. That's what I want. Nice and simple, and out of our zone." He turned back to watch the game.

"Sounds better than Gold's goon-it-up strategy," Bossy said to his linemates.

"What sounds good is putting this game away with another goal," Fryer said. "We've got to get the next one."

Kyle leaned over and patted Rocket on the helmet. "Trying to kill yourself?"

"I wanted to test the board's softness," Rocket said.

"I like the kamikaze, but let's try and last the season," Kyle said.

"Can't live forever, bro."

"Righteous words, Little Guy," Kyle said.

Rocket burst out laughing. He high-fived Kyle. Bossy and Fryer joined in.

"Let's keep our head in the game," Alvo growled. "It's not over yet."

Rocket reached for a water bottle, still giggling a bit.

Cash had the puck at the red line. Ty moved forward to pressure. Hoffer was open on the left by the boards. Cash tried to slip the puck between Ty's skates and jump around him. Ty brought his skates together and blocked it. Suddenly, there was a three-on-two. Rocket stopped laughing and got to his feet.

"Hustle back, forwards," Rocket yelled.

Ty whipped the puck to his hard-driving right winger, who carried it over the blue line and gave it back to Ty.

Ty dragged the puck on his forehand, waiting. Glassy was deep in his net.

"This is bad," Rocket said.

He'd seen Ty do this a thousand times. Two metres inside the top of the circle, with Glassy still back, Ty let it fly. He rarely missed from there. He didn't this time, either. The puck whistled over Glassy's shoulder into the top corner. Rocket slapped the top of the boards.

Bourque's line filed out.

"Get it back, Kyle. Let's go, Bourquey — all you!" Rocket shouted.

A few London Knights fans began chanting their team's name. That motivated the Axmen's supporters to get back into it.

Go Axmen Go! came raining down.

Cash smashed his stick on the ice as he came off.

"Third period, up a goal — you can't turn the puck over in the neutral zone. You've got to chip it in deep," Alvo snapped. "I can't see that again."

Cash kept his head down and shuffled to the middle of the bench.

"Quick shift. Come on, Coach!" Rocket looked into the stands. Chris and Dawn were on their feet a couple rows up. He figured they should save their breath. Gold was gone. Cash didn't have a free pass anymore. From now on a dumb play would be rewarded with a seat on the bench. Things had changed for Cash today.

Things had changed for Rocket, too. He'd gone from being kicked off the team to playing on the first line. At least for tonight. He wondered where else this hockey journey would take him.

In three seasons he'd be eligible for the NHL draft. That meant he had three years to convince the hockey world that he deserved a shot, three years to grow those three or four inches. It almost seemed like forever, but he had a lot of work to do.

The referee skated to centre and blew his whistle. The Axmen fans began to cheer even louder.

A picture of himself as a little kid flashed into his mind. He was nine, playing with Ty and Ad-man for the Oakmont Huskies. Their coach had put them together on a line for the first game. Rocket had been almost out of his mind with excitement for the game to start. As soon as the puck had dropped, he'd pleaded with his teammates to skate harder and faster. And he'd repeated two words so often that they became his line's favourite hockey expression.

He got to his feet.

"Let's motor, Axmen," he yelled. "Bring it!"

ABOUT THE AUTHOR

David Skuy spent most of his childhood playing one sport or another — hockey, soccer, football, rugby. Now he is a writer and lawyer who lives in Toronto, Ontario with his wife and two kids. He still plays hockey, coaches at minor league level, and remains a die-hard Leafs fan. He began writing the Game Time series to try to capture the competition, the challenges, the friendships and the rivalries that make sports so much fun.

His book *Undergrounders* won the Silver Birch Award in 2012. *Rocket Blues*, his first book about Bryan "Rocket" Rockwood, was a *Best Books for Kids and Teens* starred selection and is nominated for the Snow Willow Award and the Manitoba Young Readers' Choice Award.

Bryan "Rocket" Rockwood is faced with the unthinkable: being cut from the Huskies — the AAA hockey team he has played on for three years. With no other teams interested in him, Bryan reluctantly joins a AA team, the Blues, at his best friend Maddy's insistence.

Things only get worse when Rocket sees that the Blues don't take hockey seriously. Facing the Huskies in the round robin will give Rocket the chance to prove his skills, but to keep his hockey dreams — and his friends — Rocket must realize that while hockey is his passion, it is not his entire life.

ISBN 978-1-4431-3375-3

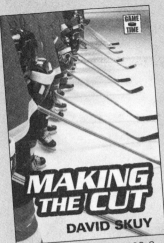

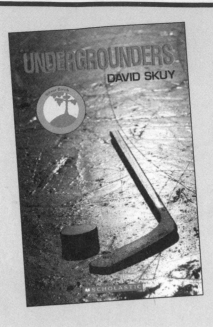

Since his mom died, Jonathon has been on his own, living on the streets. The Underground gives him a place to sleep, but it's not like having a real home or being a regular kid. That seems like an impossible dream.

Escape comes to him in the form of hockey gear. He heads to the community rink, where kids welcome him into their game and onto their team. Playing hockey makes Jonathon feel normal again, but keeping his double life a secret proves to be more difficult and dangerous than he ever could have imagined.

Winner of the Silver Birch Award

". . . sensitively written and compelling . . ."
—*CM*

ISBN 978-1-4431-0728-0